THE RICE
PAPER DIARIES

by

Francesca Rhydderch

SEREN

Seren is the book imprint of
Poetry Wales Press Ltd
57 Nolton Street, Bridgend, Wales, CF31 3AE
www.serenbooks.com
Facebook: facebook.com/SerenBooks
Twitter: @SerenBooks

ISBN: 978-1-78172-051-6

Cover image: Daniel Murtagh / Millennium Images, UK
Typesetting by Elaine Sharples
Printed by Bell and Bain, Glasgow

The publisher works with the financial assistance of
The Welsh Books Council

MIX
Paper from
responsible sources
FSC® C007785
FSC
www.fsc.org

If every departure from the native land is a small death, then every return is a resurrection.

Kica Kolbe

CONTENTS

LONDON, 1996

Marge seems to gather ill feeling around her, like the flesh that bowls out around her hips. She has a way of staring at people, and of holding their gaze when they catch her eye by mistake. She is unnerving.

She isn't much of a tea girl either. People who ask for milk get it slopped into their saucer as well as their cup. Mostly, though, they keep quiet as it is handed over. 'Thank you,' some of them say, in the same pleading tone of voice they use with the nurses. Marge takes no notice. She understands they don't mean it; what they mean is they'd like someone else to come pushing the tea trolley past their bed, someone who'll talk about the weather and call them 'dear'. Someone homely. Later they shuffle along the corridor in their dressing gowns to Elsa's side room for a chat.

'That Marge,' they say. 'She doesn't know if she's coming or going.'

But nor does Elsa, that's the problem. She's lost the shape of the day, so that the beginnings are the end and then the beginning again. By the time Marge turns up, Elsa is quite pleased to see her. She knows then that it is the afternoon, and it will soon be visiting time.

'Cup of tea?'

Marge stands in the doorway, one hand on the trolley and the other on her hips. She has put a new colour on her hair, and it's come out dark pink. Elsa doesn't know if she meant for it to come out like that. It makes her jowls look more flushed and sweaty than usual. She looks like an angry pig.

'Is it visiting time yet?' Elsa asks.

'Tea first,' says Marge. 'Want a cup?'

'Yes, please.'

Marge turns to the trolley.

'Milk, sugar?'

Elsa knows that the thick china will feel like clay against her lips, and the stewed tea will taste bad.

'You don't have a slice of lemon, do you?'

Marge frowns.

'You're mad, you are.' She has rows of thin gold hoops hanging from her nostrils. When she shakes her head the hoops shake with her.

'Just a bit of sugar, then.' Elsa pulls herself up on the metal rail at the side of the bed. Marge brings the tray-table over her lap and puts the cup and saucer down on it. For a moment, Elsa understands what it is the other patients want from Marge. There is a silence hollowing out the air between them that Elsa wants to fill. Marge reaches over to the trolley again to fetch a miniature aluminium jug. Elsa opens her mouth to remind her that she doesn't want milk, but thinks better of it.

'Biscuit?' Marge's attention seems to be taken up by something on the rooftops the other side of the window.

'No, thanks.'

'See ya,' Marge says, and she's gone. The piles of saucers and cups rattle all the way along the corridor. There's a bang as she pushes her trolley against the double doors and heaves her way towards the lift.

A nurse pokes her head round the door.

'How are you today, Elsa?' she says. She is a square woman who doesn't seem to mind bundling parcels of old people in and out of beds and baths and onto toilets and back into bed again. She is from Serbia, she told Elsa one day, when she was making her bed. 'Did you come over because of the war?' Elsa had asked. 'War? Oh, no. I am the first of my family. My husband has an MA in Business Administration,' she'd said. Today though, she has no smile and no time. It's nearly the end of her shift.

'Could I use the phone?' says Elsa.

'You have change?'

Elsa likes the precise, correct way the nurse speaks English, each vowel pushed up against its neighbouring consonant and worked hard to make the right sound.

She reaches out to the bedside cabinet for her handbag. The cupboard is on wheels and it slides away from her as she's trying to reach it. Everything in this place is on wheels, so that in the end you slip and slither your way from one thing to another. It's a wonder Elsa isn't seasick. The nurse taps her way out of the room and down the corridor towards the day room.

Elsa opens the clasp on her bag and pats her hand around inside. The light is bad in here, maybe because of the dirty windows, where the traffic fumes have settled into the corners of the frames, or perhaps the day is starting to fade earlier than it should. She yearns for the bright light of the morning, the way it used to be, at home in her kitchen. But now she wants to talk to Mari, to hear the sound of her voice close to her in the receiver. She pushes her hand deeper into the bag, feeling into the corners for her purse. She turns the bag upside down and everything tips out onto the green sheets: paper handkerchiefs, some mints (individually wrapped), a pack of cards, an old passport with clipped corners, and a bottle of pearl pink nail varnish.

'I've told you before about the nail varnish,' says the Serbian nurse, pushing the phone box in on wheels in front of her. 'I'm just going to have to take it off again tonight before the duty doctor comes round.'

Elsa puts the varnish back into her bag. The nurse will take it off, and Elsa will paint it back on again under the night lights, and so it will go on.

'I'm going to phone my daughter,' Elsa says.

'Yes, yes.' Even the nurse's smile is brisk.

Elsa opens her purse and pulls out a few twenty-pence pieces and puts them in a row on the coverlet in front of her. She breathes in its regulation, disinfectant smell. She jumps as the money drops down into the empty box below. She can hear the phone ringing at the other end, and her heart lifts and falls as she waits for the click that will tell her Mari has picked up. But it keeps on ringing until, sighing, she puts the money back in her purse.

The peace is broken by a harsh, buzzing sound. The doors to the ward open and close and people tramp past her room in small groups – their footsteps either hesitant and dutiful, or quick, too quick, resenting this intrusion into their time. She lies back on her pillow and watches their shadows moving against the blue wall of the corridor opposite, and wonders if she did remember to ask the nurse to open the window after all, because the light seems clearer, suddenly, and the birds in the plane trees outside whistle out a fierce duet with the traffic four storeys below. She'll wait a few minutes, then she'll try again.

'Oi!' A voice rises up above the others from the street, and she thinks of Marge, set free for the rest of the day, rushing to catch a bus or tube. She thinks of her swinging her haunches from side to side to make space for herself in the crowd, pulling herself up onto the 160 to Chislehurst.

'Think of a pig,' Elsa's teacher had said once at school. They'd been told to draw a map of Wales, and at nine years old Elsa hadn't known where to begin: her world then didn't stretch beyond Gwelfor and New Quay School and Towyn

Chapel next to the Memorial Hall. 'This,' said the teacher, flourishing the chalk, 'is its snout – Anglesey.' Elsa watched the chalk scraping across the blackboard and fine particles of white dust falling away as it went. 'Front legs… Llŷn Peninsula… Pembrokeshire's the hind legs… the Valleys are the rump… and Cardiff's the curly tail, before you reach England on the other side.' Something about the way she insisted on loitering at every point, taking pleasure in doing things properly, laughing at her own joke, reminded Elsa of her mother standing in the back kitchen making brawn. Once they'd eaten all they could of the pig, Elsa's mother used to turn her attention to its head. 'Put it all in,' she used to say, slicing off the cheeks and ears and dropping them with the rest of the head into the pan, along with the trotters and tail. 'That's the way to do things. Use up every scrap.' Elsa obediently followed her teacher's instructions and got on with her map, marking Cardigan Bay (the pig's belly) and New Quay (its teats) in Indian ink, her mouth watering, tasting already the thick sauce of the salted brawn that her mother or Nannon would spoon out into a serving dish for their supper when she got home.

Maybe that's why Elsa isn't completely indifferent to Marge. She reminds Elsa of home. Not Galskarth Road, Clapham, but of where she was born, in a house overlooking the sea. Gwelfor. Her mother's house. Her father's too, of course, but she always thinks of it as her mother's.

Elsa smiles. She sees pigs chasing each other up and down the hills that run down to the sea off New Quay, herds and herds of them. She loses count. She is asleep.

I

Elsa:
Hong Kong, 1940

1

Nine.

On the way up Elsa could count the steps cut into the rock. She could look at the hibiscus flowers unfolding in the morning sun, or the oblong tiles that ran in an olive-green border each side of the hospital doors. At the top she turned round as she had been told, ready to go back down again, and that was when the whole of the western district, a straggle of three and four-storey buildings running along the waterside, started to swing around in front of her. She tried to fix her gaze on something certain and unmoving, like the strip of sea that was Victoria Harbour, or the two small islands out in the water, but they refused to stay still, and her hand shook as she ran it down the rail.

She breathed in and out, counting slowly. People had told her it would take her a year to settle in Hong Kong, but she'd had to make do with nine months. She'd started to feel sick the day they'd arrived. Everything had made her nauseous – the smell of petrol on the ferries that zigzagged across the mile-wide stretch of water between Hong Kong Island and Kowloon, the champagne teas they served at the Peninsula Hotel on the other side, and the fancy dinners that she went to with Tommy at the Jockey Club.

One, two, three.

'How are you getting on?' a nurse called down from the top, impatiently. They were busy. The third-class ward was full of

Chinese women who seemed to know already how to give birth. Elsa had seen some of them walking away down Pok Fu Lam Road, holding a baby in one arm and a light bag with the other. She was starting to feel like a nuisance. It had been three days now. The nurses told her to keep moving, that's what would get the baby to shift, and she did as she was told, but nothing was happening. Tommy had been to see her and gone back to the office again.

'You need to relax,' the nurse had said. 'You're going to have a terrible labour if you don't relax.'

No one had said it would be like this. The women at the Peninsula had laughed and told her to think of England and remember that it would all be over before too long. She'd looked at them, not making sense of what they were saying, not able to believe that time was pressing in on her swollen frame, moving her forward to a point when she would turn from one person into two, and there would be no going back.

Ever since she'd arrived in Hong Kong they'd kept up a stream of advice, these over-friendly women – *and of course, you can get an amah as well as a cook; remember to turn the blinds down at midday, it's not too bad now but it's going to get unbearable before long; the other thing you'll need is really good, strong mosquito nets* – but none of them had told her she would be standing on the steps of the Queen Mary feeling alone and afraid, wanting her mother.

Four, five, six.

The pain came again. She let out a sharp breath, trying to control it, but it pushed its way up inside and overwhelmed her, so that she reached out for the rail again and cried out.

'Who has left her here like this?'

She heard a man's voice at the edges of her consciousness. Although it sounded angry, she was thankful for it. She tried to lift her head, but she stumbled forward. All she could see was the corner of a white coat and sensible shoes, good English brogues, and she felt reassured.

'How long has she been like this?' he said.

'Not long.' It was the nurse's voice, defensive. 'Baby's not moving. We had to keep her on her feet.'

Elsa felt herself being lifted onto a stretcher and the corridors of the hospital sliding past. She put her arms out to hold onto something, to keep everything still, but someone put them back in at her sides again. The gold hands on the nurse's watch close to her face moved inevitably forward, ticking silently, blocking everything else from view. Her apron smelled of carbolic soap.

'How old is she?' It was the man's voice again.

'It's none of your business how old I am.'

The man's face came closer to hers. He had red hair and freckles that had almost disappeared into his tanned face. His eyes were set so deep in their sockets it was difficult to see what colour they were.

'It's very much my business, Mrs…'

'Jones,' the nurse said. 'Twenty. First baby.'

The way she said it made Elsa think of another baby, and then another. She couldn't imagine herself walking around the Peak with a perambulator, with a newborn in the pram and a couple of toddlers in tow.

Don't worry, darling, the women had said in the Peninsula, crossing and uncrossing their legs and lighting cigarettes. *You can get someone to do that for you.*

Seven, eight, nine.

She wanted the stretcher to change direction, to take her back to the front door of the hospital and leave her there. She wanted this angry doctor's voice to go away and stop shouting orders. But the nurses wheeled her into the middle of a bright, bare room that hurt her eyes. They lifted her onto a bed and switched on a light above her head. She looked up and saw her face reflected in its metal frame, her features young and formless.

'I'm Dr Campbell,' the man said. 'We're just giving you something for the pain.' One of his fingers caught her hair as he turned towards the table behind him.

The nurse squeezed Elsa's arm tight and put a needle in.

The doctor came back to the bed and bent over her.

'Where's your husband?'

'At the customs building,' she said.

'Connaught Road?'

His face seemed very close to hers again.

'Yes. Why?'

'I need to send someone down right away to get his signature on these forms.'

'What forms?'

'There's a new operation they've started doing, in America.'

She struggled to sit up, but he put a hand on her shoulder until she lay back down.

'Is everything all right?' she asked.

'I'm doing my best to make it all right.' His voice had lost its harsh edges, but the look on his face didn't make her feel any better. He glanced away as he held the stethoscope to her chest and listened. She stared at the outer rim of his ear, at the perfect curve of skin and cartilage. When he looked straight at her again everything balanced out, the oversized ears, long nose and deep-cut cheekbones. She wondered if he could hear the baby's heartbeat flickering under her skin, like a trapped moth beating its wings senselessly as it tried to get out.

A hot line burned its way across her chest. They told her not to look down so she looked up, and saw everything reflected in the metal edge of the light. She saw the doctor pick up a knife and a sliver of red racing across her stomach.

She saw his gloved fingers pulling the flesh back. She watched as a head attached to four small frog legs was lifted out.

She waited, and wondered what she was waiting for.

'You'll need a trousseau,' Nannon had said, when Elsa had told her she was getting married and going to Hong Kong. 'And there's the heat to consider. Let's have a think.'

She leaned over the glass counter. She picked up a smooth piece of tailor's chalk and set to writing notes to herself on the back of a satin offcut.

That was Nannon all over. Whatever the occasion – a wedding, baptism, or homecoming – she would look it up in one of her books, and write out a list. Once she'd finished she would leave them lying around, only to find them later, abandoned under the sewing machine, or next to the till. She'd read them through, perplexed, saying, 'Whatever was that all about? What on earth would I have been making with tulle *and* bengaline?' as if the mysteries of her past self were too fragmented for her even to begin to stitch them back together. Finally she lowered her eyebrows, the furrows on her forehead disappeared, and she immersed herself in the certainties of the present again.

'How hot is it out there, anyway? In summer, I mean?'

'Very?' Elsa shrugged her shoulders. 'I'm not sure.' She thought of all the things she didn't know yet about Hong Kong.

Nannon pulled open the shallow drawers under the counter. She brought out copies of fashion magazines and a dog-eared manual on etiquette. Elsa used to flinch when Nannon looked things up in that book, licking her index finger and riffling through the pages until she landed on the one she wanted. The next stage would be Elsa in her petticoat and Nannon with a mouthful of pins, until whatever it was – Elsa's school uniform, or a dress for her first dinner dance – was sewn together and ironed out and hung up.

This time was no exception. No matter that Elsa was getting married before her, and going to the other side of the world. Growing up at last. Nannon was going to see Elsa right, she said. Do them both proud.

She started on one of her lists, and Elsa waited, knowing better than to interrupt. The shop smelled of Nannon, the way she smelled first thing in the morning when she'd splashed her face with lavender water and combed her hair out and put it up in a bun on the top of her head. She smelled of camphor and roses and freshly baked biscuits.

'The average bride will also need three to four house dresses,' – Nannon's forehead wrinkled up again as she read aloud from the book – 'two or three tea aprons, and one large apron for kitchen work. The bride who expects to entertain women friends extensively and who moves in an extravagant set should also have a tea gown or lounging pajamas.'

'Lounging pajamas it is, then,' she said, setting her chalk down on the counter decisively. 'Whatever they might be.' She sniffed, reaching for her tape measure.

Elsa didn't wear the pajamas, or the aprons. In Hong Kong everyone had a cook for lunch and went out for dinner. The aprons hung on the back of the kitchen door. Nannon had made them out of one of their mother's old dresses, one of Elsa's favourites, a pale blue gingham, serviceable and summery, intended Elsa knew to remind her of their mother without recalling the dark, frozen memory of losing her.

When Elsa, trying to distract herself, told her Hong Kong friends that at home men dressed up for New Year in sheets and ribbons and carried a horse's skull from house to house, as a kind of prank played on neighbours to add to the evening's entertainment, they forgot their manners and let out huge belly laughs. 'Yes, they call it the Mari Lwyd, the horse,' Elsa said, getting quite carried away, enjoying her audience, and they tittered again, and she realised they weren't laughing with her, and she stopped talking.

And she remembered that when her mother was ill no one had told her what was happening, at first. She sat in the kitchen excited because it was New Year's Eve, listening to Megan, the girl who came in to help with the washing and scrubbing, talking about the Mari Lwyd.

'Is it a real horse?' Elsa asked. 'Or a ghost?'

Megan laughed, stirring a pot on the range.

'Neither. It's men dressed up, it is. They put a big white sheet over their heads and one of them carries a horse's skull hung with ribbons all colours, and when you open the door they want to give you a fright. Just for fun.'

Megan had been too cheerful, far more cheerful than usual. Usually she had a face like a mangle, their father said, but on that day she'd been making an effort to appear lively, perhaps under orders. Everything in the kitchen was too cosy and warm. In Elsa's memory every surface shines: the table, the row of pans hanging over the range, the little coffee pot from Mexico that Elsa loves so much. And their mother, lying back in bed upstairs, her cheeks flushed and her hair out around her on the pillow, making her look young, not like someone about to die.

But still Elsa had no idea. Her father had been home for longer than usual, it was true, so she'd had time to get used to him again, to the English words that he scattered like seeds through the tilled rows of his Welsh, and to wonder what it meant, some of it, that was too quick for her. All she knew was that their mother was out of sorts, and that she was in bed.

And then, in her memory of it at least, Megan is gone, and

her father is gone and she is sitting alone in the kitchen, listening to the *cawl* bubble in its pot. There is a knock at the back door and she rushes to open it, looking forward to the fun and the surprise and the pretty ribbons, and calling *Mammy, Mammy, everyone, come and see, what fun*, and then the door is open and the dressed-up horse looks like a real dead horse, his teeth gnashing in his skull and she is terrified and screams and screams and her father is crying out harshly upstairs in a voice she has never heard before, and Nannon, too tall and thin, comes downstairs and puts her finger to her lips and takes Elsa to see their mother lying still with her eyes open and the windows shut and their father with his back turned away from them. Her mother's face was flat on the pillow, and her lips had ridden up a little back off her teeth, showing a perfect row of white pearls with serrated edges.

That was the last time anyone called at Gwelfor on New Year's Eve. Nannon made up their black dresses from one of her fashion magazines with Elsa at her side, passing her the pins and thread, neither of them saying a word. Although Elsa was only nine, she understood well enough. How could Nannon even begin to prick the surface of their loss? There was no manual for that.

Elsa listened to the rhythmic turn of the fan above the light. She looked at the top of the doctor's head, as he moved over to a small side table with a glaring spotlight above it. She turned to see what was going on, but the nurses told her not to.

In the room next door a baby yowled. Cars passed occasionally on the road below that led to Repulse Bay. Footsteps hurried along corridors with polished linoleum floors.

The fan hanging from the ceiling cut through the air a few more times, and then stopped. Someone had switched it off. The doctor and two nurses were standing over at the small table, looking into a towel spread out under the light, like a half-opened package. No one was saying anything.

She counted without breathing. She hadn't expected this.

Seven, eight, nine.

Silence.

2

When her mother had died, Elsa had spent days sitting at the kitchen table. She'd read books, practised her looped handwriting and looked at the food that Nannon made. Sometimes she fell asleep there, elbows pushed out and her head resting on her forearms, so that her face felt creased and uncomfortable when she woke up. Nannon understood, and said nothing. She took the food away and left Elsa to sit at the table. Their mother had called herself a proper New Quay woman (although she had always smiled when she said 'proper': *Let the men travel to Peru, or round Cape Horn, or to Australia and back*, she said); her four-cornered world was this Pembroke table, with a drawer in its side for cutlery, and flaps that could be folded away. It wasn't a kitchen table, not really, it was too delicate and portable for that, but their mother had made it hers. She kept the flaps propped open and used it to pluck chickens, roll out pastry, make apple jelly, and to do the accounts. When they needed to eat she took a fresh tablecloth out and unfolded it and flicked it open so that its corners flew up into the air before landing on the table, and Elsa used to set out the cutlery, big pieces of silver with heavy handles. If there was ironing to be done, her mother put an old blanket over it while the iron heated up on the range behind her. When their father came home (once, maybe twice a year, like other 'proper' New Quay men, except that sometimes the proper New Quay men didn't come back at all, not if they contracted yellow fever in Mauritius or malaria in Africa), it was on this table that his presents were tumbled out for them to pore over: wooden elephants from Kenya the size of Elsa's dolls, with tusks made of real bone, Japanese tea sets, music boxes with lacquered tops.

After the funeral the kitchen table became Elsa's centre of gravity too. While Nannon went for long walks, collecting wild flowers to take up to their mother's grave, Elsa ran her hands over the scored surface of the table, reading its bleached cracks like the lifelines on a handprint that became more difficult to distinguish as time went on, but never disappeared entirely.

When she came to Hong Kong with Tommy, she wanted to bring the table with her, to get it shipped over with the rest of her things, and Tommy said yes, anything she wanted she could have and that he would arrange it, but in the end she was afraid of something happening to it, and she left it behind with Nannon. It would have been too big for their apartment, anyway. The kitchen here had a formica table that rippled like marble, but Elsa couldn't sit at it now, in any case, because Wang was having his lunch.

She sat on the terrace watching the skiffs down in the harbour. Everything seemed very small from up here. The spacious grounds of their apartment were studded with trees which muffled the sounds that rose up to the Peak from the city below. She had found it suffocating when they first moved here – she was used to New Quay's terraces of houses set close to each other with no room for trees, unless the gardens behind had been levelled into the hill. She liked seeing and hearing the sea up close. But she was glad to be hidden away here now; she didn't much care about their smart address, but she could stay away from the whist drives and parties and shows, and wait for the empty feeling inside her to recede.

But it didn't. Every day she felt more lethargic. Every time she moved, she felt the weight of herself as a single human unit, and the echo of something that wasn't there. It was easier to stay still.

'We can have another one as soon as you like,' Tommy whispered to her in bed at night, but she pulled away.

He tried other tactics, like asking Wang to sort out the nursery, turn it back into her dressing room while she was downtown having her hair done, but they had all ended badly.

'Meet me for lunch?' he'd said, before Wang drove him down to the customs building that morning.

She'd shaken her head.

When the doorbell went, Elsa didn't get up to answer it. She didn't want to talk to the neighbours. Passing the time of day was something she preferred to do alone now, each breath taking her further away from that moment when they'd lifted the baby out and found that he was dead.

The nurses hadn't wanted to let her see him, but Oscar Campbell had.

He'd looked tiny, and agitated, as if he'd been crying for a long time but no one had come to him. His fists were tightly curled together. She'd reached out and put her hand on his cheek. It was still warm; white mucus covered his features in a sticky web. His eyes were shut.

She knew Tommy was cross with the doctor for letting her see him.

'What purpose did you think it would serve?' she'd heard him saying.

'I did what I thought was best.'

'And what makes you think this was for the best?'

'She can draw a line under it now.'

She could see why Tommy was angry, though. It had drawn a line between them too. She had seen their baby and he hadn't. She could dwell on things if she wanted to. She'd given him a name, although nobody else knew about it, even Tommy, and sometimes she whispered to herself as if she were talking to him. *Come along Harry, time for your nap*, or *Time for your bath*, or *Let's go out for a walk now, Harry*. She could sit for a whole morning and reassemble him in her imagination. She could think of what she would have been doing first thing, when he would have had his feeds, or a clean nappy, or been carried up and down the verandah. If she sat here and walked her way through the day in her imagination, it was almost as good as him being there.

Tommy soon put a stop to that, though.

'Wang says you haven't moved all day.'

'Wang isn't my nurse, he's my driver.'

'He says you haven't eaten anything either.'

The doorbell went again. Tommy said that drivers didn't need to hear, but Elsa wished that Wang wasn't quite so deaf. She was tired of shouting instructions at him. When she opened the front door there was a Chinese woman standing in the hall. Her eyes looked large in her face, and her hair was plaited elaborately and pinned up around her head.

'Miss?' she said.

'What is it?'

'You wanted to see me?'

Elsa looked at her, shaking her head.

'We have an appointment,' the woman ventured. 'Wang said you have a vacancy, and I was told to come today.'

Trying to remember her way back to a time before the baby was like walking down from the Peak on the one winding road in the dark, getting lost under the candlenut trees.

'Your services are no longer required.'

'What?'

'There is no baby, all right?' Elsa raised her voice. 'So you can go back down to wherever you came from and leave me alone.'

She slammed the door and went out onto the terrace. It was a clear day, despite the heat, and she could see over to the other side of Kowloon, where the buildings stopped and a row of hills stood up straight behind. The water in the harbour changed colour through the day, pale and hazy at first, a deep blue by the afternoon, and then a milky yellow just before sunset. If the weather was good and they had a free evening ahead of them, Tommy sometimes got Wang to drive them over the Peak and along the coast a little way. As twilight fell, they would often sit and watch the fishermen set to work. Two junks with a net suspended between them sailed in one direction, and a small *sampan* carrying kerosene lamps made for the gap between them. The light attracted the fish, Tommy said, and they went straight into the nets. She wanted to go for a spin that way now, with Wang driving quickly through the villages where people would look at her in the car as she passed, and not know anything of her pain, and she could look back at them through the glass, and feel nothing.

She went to the kitchen.

'Ah Wang?'

Wang looked up, startled.

The formica table had been moved against the wall. He was sitting on the bamboo mat in the centre of the room. The woman who'd come to call was sitting with him. She held a patterned china cup between her fingers and sipped, delicately. There was a sweet smell in the air.

'Excuse us, please,' he said.

'No, it's fine. Don't get up.'

'This is my cousin, Lam,' he said. 'The captain asked her to come... anyway.'

'I understand,' she said. She looked at the woman sitting cross-legged on the floor. She felt embarrassed, standing over them like this, but didn't want to sit down, either.

'Please accept my apologies. I was very rude to you earlier,' she said to the woman.

'I'm sorry,' the woman said. 'You lost your baby.'

It was the first time someone had said it to her, made it real.

'Captain Jones thought I could help. Keep you company until you want to go out again.'

'I'd like that. Please, finish your tea and then we can talk in the living room.'

'Yes, Miss.' Lam lifted her teacup again.

Elsa went back to the living room and onto the verandah. She stood in the glare of the sunlight, and let it burn her skin. She looked at the poinsettia flowers glowing red against the blue glaze of their pots, and breathed in the cool smell of the tree shade on the hill behind. While she was waiting for Lam to come and sit with her, she read Nannon's letter again. They arrived once a week, on the dot. She stared at the neat handwriting, blowsy in places. *Rain again this morning, and cool. You'd never say it was June. The rapeseed is out though, big bold stripes of it across the fields, thick as butter.*

3

Every time they rounded a corner Elsa was swung from one side of the Bentley to the other, although Wang was driving slowly and the road wasn't busy.

'Surprise for Captain Jones?' he asked.

'Yes, Ah Wang.'

Tommy had left that morning without saying goodbye.

'All right, if you won't come with me, I'm going on my own,' he'd said. 'Don't expect me back until late.'

After he'd gone, Elsa had sat in her dressing room for a long time, next to where the cot had been. The blind was drawn against the sun, and she sat in a half-light, her senses dulled. She pictured Tommy sitting with Ronald and Liz on the terrace at the Jockey Club, lighting cigarettes for the women around the table, smoke and perfume heavy in the air above them. She knew the kind of woman who would come and pull out the empty seat next to him, murmuring 'Do you mind?' He would jump up and push her chair in for her and smile and not notice the way she looked at him, because women always looked at Tommy like that. The debutante types would never have the courage even to speak to him: they would just blush and stare, until in the end, feeling watched, he would look round, at which they'd blush again and the sea would glimmer in the harbour behind them and Tommy would smile back without thinking about it. The married ones, who talked to other women about children's diets and charity dos, would look at him twice too, and then back at their own husbands, before picking up the conversation where they'd left off, viciously, as if they were pulling a stray thread out of a skirt. It was the older, single women she had to look out for, the ones who'd kept their figures and their bank balances and had no need of a man, but didn't mind a little light entertainment from time to time. But Tommy always said there was no other woman for him. He'd turn to their friends round the table and say that there was no other woman in Hong Kong who could speak Welsh half as well as she could. Everyone laughed, and Elsa would let herself tip over into the familiar cadences of the well-worn joke and laugh too, while Tommy would put his hand over hers – 'Is there, my *cariad*?'

But Tommy had stopped making wisecracks, and Elsa had stopped laughing at everything he said. *Losing a baby is no joke*, she imagined the mumsy women saying to him. *She won't ever be quite the same, you know that*, one hand on his shoulder.

She got out of the car as Wang held the door open for her, the engine still running, and Happy Valley spinning out in a circle around her: the smoothly mown grass, the wide blue sky, the Peak falling sharply away behind.

'Don't wait for me, Ah Wang.'

He looked disappointed. Lam said there was nothing Wang liked better than an afternoon spent sitting in the car waiting, polishing the dashboard. She said it with disdain, before remembering that she was Elsa's servant, and putting her hand over her mouth, and saying that she had work to do. But the last time Elsa had asked her to keep her company on the terrace she had stayed longer than usual, making the afternoon pass more quickly.

The bar was crowded and hot. Men stood about with a glass in one hand and race lists and a cigarette or pipe in the other. One or two of them eyed Elsa through the smoke. Everyone looked too warm.

She passed one of Tommy's friends from the customs building; he smiled at her and she smiled back, watching as the sheen of his skin disappeared into the lines around his eyes. She felt someone's warm breath on the back of her neck as she untangled herself from one group of people and gently pushed her way through another – 'Excuse me, please.' She passed a table of women who were sitting around a low coffee table, passing a lighter round. They spoke in full, authoritative voices.

'But for God's sake,' one of them drawled. 'Look around you. Everything's just fine.'

The woman next to her took her turn with the lighter, sucking in a deep first draw until the cigarette took, snapping the lighter shut when she was done.

'I'm glad I'm just passing through. I think you should all get out pronto.'

Liz didn't seem surprised to see Elsa. She was woozy already.

'Get us another drink, Ronald, there's a dear.' She held up her empty glass.

Ronald brought Elsa a whisky and soda that numbed the back of her tongue. Liz sat up in her chair and tapped Ronald's knee.

'Ronnie and I have got some news, haven't we?'

'Sure have,' Ronnie said. He sent a flickering look in the direction of the bar, where a group of young women were standing around, smoothing out their skirts and waiting for the races to begin.

'What is it?' Elsa asked, although the flip in her stomach made her think she might know what it was already.

'Ronnie and I are going to have a baby,' Liz said, loudly enough for the group on the next table to hear. People turned round and smiled politely, raising their champagne glasses.

'That's wonderful.' Elsa tried to sound excited but her voice came out dull and flat. 'I'm pleased for you Lizzie, I really am.'

'It'll all go right for you next time, you'll see.' Lizzie touched her on the shoulder.

Perhaps some women were cut out for motherhood and not others. Liz was the kind of woman whose soft, giving flesh seemed made for it. Perhaps Elsa was too tense, always so uptight, as Tommy'd said that morning. She still wondered why the baby's hands had been clenched, as if he'd known all along that something was wrong, that it wasn't ever going to go right. Elsa had spent nine carefree months enjoying herself, out sightseeing like a tourist, walking past blue-and-gold macaws in the bird market, row upon row of them, feathers floating in the air around her; buying outrageous bouquets at the flower stall, wrapped up in scarlet twine, thinking that Hong Kong was bold and bright and just the way it should be. She'd been thinking all the time about this being the beginning of things, while Harry had known all along that it was the end. Perhaps he had been the only one to know. Apart from the doctor. *He'd* known straightaway.

Nannon had made a list for a layette and posted it to her airmail, but it had got lost in the post and hadn't reached her, not until she got back from the hospital. She'd sat in bed with the blinds drawn, examining it over and over, trying to crack it like some kind of secret code, Nannon's absolute belief that babies arrive in this world, and when they do, they need booties and Turkish towels.

'Where's Tommy?' she said to Liz.

'The other end of the bar.' Liz's hand was still pressed down on Ronald's knee, as if to make sure he didn't get up and go over to the bar himself.

Elsa craned her neck around the groups of hips and waists and hands in pockets, until she saw Tommy, his back against the wall and an arm stretched out along the bar, one foot resting on the gold rail that ran at his feet all the way round to the door. He was laughing. A woman with dark hair down her back and a plain woollen dress that looked out of place amongst all the organza and crepe stood between him and everyone else. Elsa watched Tommy's face. He was listening as the woman talked. She was gesticulating affectedly, probably speaking quietly so he had to bend towards her and concentrate to catch what she was saying. He stopped smiling suddenly, and started nodding, as if she was telling him something he knew and he agreed with her. The woman put an arm on the lapel of his jacket and was starting to talk more quickly and urgently as Elsa came up behind her.

'Elsa,' Tommy interrupted the woman and reached out to draw Elsa into the middle of their twosome. He put both arms around her and pulled her to him. One of the buttons on his shirt had come undone and Elsa could feel his hot skin against hers.

'Elsa, this is Miss Mimi Forsyth. She's a journalist.'

The woman was older than she looked from behind; there were streaks of grey in her hair and fine lines of black kohl had smudged a little around her eyes. 'Pleased to meet you,' Elsa said, stretching out one arm to shake her hand.

'Enjoying Hong Kong, Mrs Jones?'

The journalist was looking at Tommy and not Elsa.

'It's quite a home from home.' Elsa tried to sound polite. 'What about you? What brings you here?'

The woman answered reluctantly, as if she'd rather make eyes at Tommy all day.

'There's going to be a war and I'm here to report on it.'

Elsa looked over at Tommy, expecting to see one of his social grimaces in place, accompanied by a comment about the Japs getting too big for their boots. But he just took his arm off the bar and raised it, as if to stop the rush of words that might follow, or to surrender to them, Elsa didn't know which. Elsa wondered how well he knew this journalist.

'Mimi, don't you think you're being a bit jumpy about all this?' He'd stopped smiling.

'Things are getting more serious, Tom.' She said his name as if she owned it, tucking her hair back over her ears as she spoke. She looked directly at him as if Elsa wasn't there, challenging him to disagree with her.

'There are bombs in London,' Elsa said. 'Not here.'

She had no notion of how bombs might sound, or the havoc they might make, apart from the odd story from back home that she'd picked up in the Hong Kong dailies. All that Nannon had to say about it in her letters was that that the price of eggs and sugar had gone up again.

'How well do you know the Pacific?' said Mimi.

Nannon would have known how to deal with a woman like this. *Drama queen.*

'So is that what you're doing, Miss Forsyth?' Elsa said. 'Sitting in an office writing stories about the war in Europe?'

'I can't tell you half of what I'm doing. It's classified. I can't even tell Tommy.' It was there again, her husband's name spread out like a warm palm around this woman.

She wondered if Harry had been dead when they'd lifted him out, or if his heart had stopped beating on the examination table. No one had said much afterwards, just how sorry they were, as if, now that it had happened, it wasn't really important to know how, or why. But those were the details that Elsa wanted to keep, like pressed flowers that would fall out of the pages of a book later on, the colour and sap drained out of them, but still reminding her of the short, dark life he'd lived inside her. This journalist wouldn't understand.

Tommy cleared his throat.

'First race in five minutes, ladies and gentlemen!' someone shouted down the bar. People started to wander through to the box outside in threes and fours.

They were among the last to leave, and Tommy turned to thank the waiter who was holding the door open for them.

'Hello, Dai, my man!' Tommy laughed, clapping him on the back, and the boy laughed back, not knowing that he looked comical in his stiffly starched shirt that was too big for him. No one was invisible to Tommy. He talked to everyone as if they were his friend, and not in that polite way that expects no answer. People's faces opened up when he spoke to them, even if he was still laughing at some joke that he first made six months ago.

'Yes.' The boy had his hand on the door. 'Dai is a good Welsh name!' he said, smiling. 'Good afternoon, Captain.'

'Goodbye, Dai Lo,' Elsa said as she passed him, in good spirits again now that Mimi Forsyth had gone on ahead. 'Nice to see you again.'

'Yes, Mrs Captain. Goodbye.'

As Tommy closed the door behind them Elsa caught a glimpse of Dai Lo running a cloth over the ring marks and cigarette burns that had pushed their way through the tabletops like spores. He told her once that he loved the races.

Tommy was in a good mood. He and Ronald were doing well, and there was one race to go. Elsa could see the starter pistol held up in the air, waiting for the signal. That moment, as his fingers pulled the trigger, stretched out like elastic, so that later all Elsa would remember of this afternoon would be the straw roughly strewn underfoot, the crouched jockeys poised for the off, and the startled horses jumping one after the other. Two minutes later, after a flash of silky brown muscles, it was over.

'Where have Ron and Liz got to?'

Tommy was pushing a good handful of dollar bills into his wallet.

Elsa caught sight of them coming out of the clubhouse. Liz looked untidy and happy. Tommy put his arm around Elsa, and they walked over to Ronald's car.

'I'm so pleased you came today,' he said to her. The air was much cooler now, and she was glad of his arm on her shoulder.

A man walked past them the other way, back into the clubhouse. He wore a smart suit, and had his hair combed back off his face.

'Was that Oscar Campbell?'

'I didn't see. I don't think so,' said Tommy, pulling her back towards him and kissing her on the neck as he held the car door open for her.

Ronnie drove along Sassoon Road, where rows of shoe shops rubbed up against each other, and Elsa waited for Tommy to make a joke about the pairs of shoes lined up at the bottom of her wardrobe. But he hadn't even noticed them. He was talking in a quiet, quick voice to Ronnie, and Ronnie was nodding in silence, his eyes in the mirror sliding from left to right along the pavements.

The car passed a chemist's with a bottled embryo on display, so small and jellied Elsa found it hard to believe it would ever have grown into a real baby. Liz held a handkerchief against her mouth. A beggar pushed his hand through the open window at one of the intersections – 'Please, please,' – frightening both of them and making Ronald swear.

'For God's sake Liz, close the window,' he said.

And then they turned the corner past the hairdresser's and Jimmy's café, and the neon lights of the city began to fade into a glowing mass below them.

Tommy winked at Elsa over his shoulder.

'Won't be long now,' he said.

4

It was only once Elsa had put one foot on the stairs leading to the upper deck of the tram that she realised her mistake. Lam hung back, pointing to the Chinese sign next to the driver.

'I can't come up there. Chinese sit downstairs. You go up, and I'll let you know when we need to get off.'

The windows were open at each side, letting in a cross-draught that carried with it the smell of fish. On the street below, long, thin shops were fronted by metal trays piled high with *paak tsoi*, gnarled bulbs of ginger, sweet potatoes, and green grapefruit. A butcher stood over a chopping board, a cleaver in one hand and the other pinning a fish to the board. It flapped up and down helplessly, first head, then tail, from one end to the other. He struck it over the head with the handle of the knife and then started gutting it. It was still moving, the transparent white fin on its side thrashing up and down.

'Des Voeux Road, Mrs Jones.'

Lam said it quietly enough, but her voice carried up the stairs. Elsa held onto the metal pole and pulled herself to her feet. Lam was waiting for her on the pavement.

'Where's the shop?'

They were making their way through the crowds of people: men pushing small trolleys loaded with pallets, old women stooped over bamboo baskets, and children careering around in-between them.

'Bonham Road. Just round the corner.'

Elsa felt uncomfortable. She could sense the Chinese looking at her, noting her presence. Although she was wearing flat shoes, she still felt too tall. She was glad when they turned off the main road and walked up a steep hill away from the crowds.

'This is it,' said Lam, turning into a shop with red-and-gold paper lanterns hanging outside.

A man and woman were sitting on the floor of the dim interior, sewing. Their hands moved up and down in time with each other, as if they were conducting an unseen orchestra. They were working on a dress made of embroidered silk: he was attending to the hem, while she was sewing white piping into the high collar. As they moved along the garment, they looked up at each other, each making sure that the other wasn't moving too quickly, or about to tug the material without warning.

As Elsa got used to the light, the shapes of their lined faces became clearer. The old woman looked like Wang, although she seemed old to be his mother. Elsa sat down straightaway, to avoid the awkwardness of them putting their work aside and getting to their feet, but they looked at her in surprise, and moved away, as if she had sat too close to them.

'Very pleased to meet you both,' she said.

They looked back at her.

Lam sat next to Elsa, crossing her legs with an ease Elsa couldn't find. She said something to the old couple in what must be Cantonese, or Mandarin maybe. Tommy would know. They smiled at Elsa then.

'They don't speak English,' Lam said to her. 'They've been ten years in Hong Kong but they still prefer our language.'

Elsa didn't know what she had expected – somewhere larger, with a counter that you could sit at, maybe. In Bristol House Nannon's counter doubled up as a table. If she had time she made a cup of tea for her customers, saying, 'Now then, let's have a nice chat.' Before ten minutes had gone by the customer would have

43

forgotten the alterations they came in with and would be poring over patterns for a dressy wrap and thinking about how often they would wear it and how much it would cost. They would have an image of themselves in their mind's eye that would please them for once, and Nannon would know exactly how to capture that image, breaking off from the usual chit-chat to point out the wrap's sequin ties, tapping a fingernail on the folded-out page. 'See, that's the detail that makes it, in my opinion. That would stand out lovely under the lights, anywhere. Not too dressy, though, is it? Classy, I'd call it.'

Lam talked again swiftly to the man and woman, a little sharply, it seemed to Elsa, and they got up on their feet, rubbing their stiff joints as they did so, and the old woman gestured for Elsa to follow her behind a curtain to a recessed area at the back of the shop. She measured Elsa with quick fingers, the tape measure hardly touching her, even through her clothes. She talked loudly to Lam through the curtain. Elsa looked at her as she spoke, but her face was blank, waiting for Lam's reply.

'She's asking what kind of style you want,' said Lam. 'Would you like to call back with some pictures, a catalogue maybe?'

'Tell her that I trust her to make me a nice frock. Any style, any colour.'

Elsa came out from behind the curtain. People going past the shop looked twice when they saw her standing there. She was starting to feel as if she was taking up too much room, and she took a step out onto the street, almost bumping into a woman going past, a baby strapped tightly to her back, its black pigtail swaying up and down as she walked. Nothing could happen to them if you kept them close like that, she thought.

'She says she will choose pink, a deep pink, to go with your dark hair. It will be ready by the end of the week.'

'So soon? There's no need.'

'Yes, yes, by Friday,' Lam said, coming out onto the pavement as well.

44

The Wangs bowed, showing the shiny tops of their heads through fine strands of grey hair, and settled down to their work again, sitting side by side, fingers moving in and out of the material, fresh and soft as a newly slaughtered fish, its fragile white bones all on show.

'Is there somewhere we can have lunch?'

Elsa didn't want to go back to the apartment just yet. She'd rather wait until Tommy was due home from work.

Lam slowed down.

'This way,' she said.

The restaurant was on the corner of a block, spread over three floors, with too much warm air circulating between the crowded tables. People were sitting in big family groups, and some of the men were reading newspapers.

Elsa was glad of the cool breeze by the window. She took her hat off and looked out at the craned boats and *sampans* jostling against each other for space on the quay. There must have been twenty people on the table next to them, dressed smartly. Children were playing hide-and-seek on all fours, in and out of the drapes of the tablecloth. From time to time one of them came out and said something to their parents and went back again, and as the tablecloth was lifted Elsa saw that they were playing with spinning tops, staring at the blur the colourful tops made as they whirled around.

A waitress brought a tray filled with covered bamboo pans and set them out on the table. Lam took off the lids and pointed to the contents of each in turn with her chopsticks.

'Bean curd, fried noodles, steamed fish with mushroom, vegetable dumplings.'

Elsa helped herself to a little from each pan. She saw the children from the table next to them watching her as the dumplings fell off her chopsticks and she had to try again and again. She laughed.

'How on earth do you do it?'

45

Lam smiled and shook her head.

'Here, let me help you.'

They looked out over the harbour as they ate. A spinning top jumped out from under the table next to them. One of the boys crept over, head down, put an arm out to retrieve it, and scuttled away. His mother was eating dragon fruit with chopsticks. Bottles of brandy were being brought to the table. Men raised their glasses and shouted '*Yam sing!*' before draining them and topping them up again and again.

'It's a wedding party,' Lam said.

The bride and groom looked as if their cheeks must hurt from all the smiling. Elsa tried to catch Lam's eye, to share the joke, but she had seemed to have shifted into one of her closed-up moods, a distant look on her face. She was staring at a man and woman seated to the other side of them. The woman was giggling, leaning into the man. He had a broad smile that was wide enough for everyone. American, at a guess, thought Elsa, listening to his accent. The skin hung slackly off his jaw, perhaps because he was a little overweight, although he was young, not much older than Elsa. The Chinese girl sitting next to him had a strange smile pasted to her face, bright and plastic like one of the illuminated shop signs on Des Voeux Road. The man took his chopsticks and passed them to her; she broke them open for him and handed them back. Lam eyed the Chinese girl coldly, as if she were a goose strung up for sale in the butcher's on the street outside. The man noticed nothing. He shuttled his beer across the tablecloth, passing the bottle from one hand to the other. Each time he moved, Elsa caught sight of a line of scarlet flesh above the collar of his shirt where he'd caught the sun.

Elsa wanted to ask Lam what she did on her day off, if she came to places like this with men like that, but she knew that Lam would be embarrassed, and would say nothing, covering her mouth with her hand.

'Do you get homesick sometimes?' she said instead.

All around them, the dribs and drabs of conversation on other tables were starting to slow down. At the wedding party table a small child sat curled up on a woman's shoes, one thumb in his mouth and the side of his cheek pressed against her leg.

'Homesick? What's that?'

Lam tidied the bamboo pans, putting their lids back on and setting them at the edge of the table ready for the waitress.

'I mean, do you miss your home? Where is your home?'

Elsa put a ten-dollar note next to the dirty dishes.

'Keep the change,' she said to the waitress.

The waitress bowed her head and slipped the note into her apron.

'Canton? I haven't been there for three years.'

Lam's answer was just what Elsa had come to expect: neither a yes nor a no, and yet there was something complete and self-contained about it, like Lam herself.

It was cooler on the street, but the pavements were still crowded. Elsa followed Lam as she stepped round men pulling trolleys and rickshaws, and wide, shallow dishes of chickpeas drying in the sun. She tried to move as lightly as Lam did, balancing her weight in order to skip round all these hurdles in one graceful movement. They were about to cross the road to a tram stop when a car pulled up.

'What on earth are you doing here on your own?' Lizzie called over. Ronnie sat next to her in the driver's seat, wearing sunglasses and looking straight ahead.

'I'm not on my own,' Elsa said.

'Hadn't you better hop in? We'll run you home.'

Elsa turned back to Lam.

'Don't rush back. I won't need you until six.'

Lam looked pleased, then, for the first time that day. Elsa got into the car and they pulled away down Des Voeux Road, overtaking the trams. Lam was still standing on the pavement, a blank look on her face again. Everything around her was moving and gathering pace backwards as the car sped off: the triangles of the bamboo hats in the shop behind her, the yellow mangoes on the fruit stall on the other side, the long dark alleyway to her left that ran the length of the block. For a moment they came together like a symphony, a final chord, and then Lam turned to go and they fell away from her again.

'You look tired,' Liz said.

'I've had a busy day, that's all.'

'You don't have to come to this do if you don't feel up to it.'

'I'll be better by the end of the week. I wouldn't miss your birthday for anything, Ronnie.'

'Thank you, honey,' he said, blowing his cigarette smoke out of the window. 'It's going to be a good one.'

Liz laughed, looking sideways at herself in the wing mirror. 'There'll be plenty of people and plenty of fizz; I've made sure of that.'

The car stopped for a moment at a junction. Alongside them a man stooped over a grave in the steep-sided Chinese cemetery. He had a small brush in one hand and a pan in the other. Then Ronnie put his foot down again, turning up onto the road for the Peak, and everything around them disappeared into a blur of trees and sky.

5

'What's wrong?' Tommy was looking in the mirror, adjusting his bow tie.

'Nothing. I fell asleep after lunch and had a bad dream, that's all.'

'We'd better get going.'

Victoria Harbour was calm under a grey sky. No one would guess at the storm Elsa had dreamed of, the waves rising up out of the harbour and crashing over the hotels and shops and people all along the waterfront. She'd dreamed they were sitting in the Peninsula when the water rolled into the big windows, making them crack and splinter into jagged pieces that came rushing on a wave of water towards her, cutting her hands. She shouted and screamed and held her arms up, the blood running, but no one took any notice. They carried on just as before, as if this was only happening to her. And then she woke up and realised that it was.

Elsa hesitated before stepping off the quay onto the boat. There was a moment when she felt everything moving beneath her, the gangplank under one foot and the quay under the other, but then Tommy took her hand and the feeling of panic was stilled.

As the *sampan* turned back on itself to face Kowloon the evening sun caught its pewter-coloured sails, opened out symmetrically like butterfly wings. Elsa was struck by how flat the land was on the waterfront. It wasn't inconceivable that the Peninsula Hotel or any of the other smart places on the other side of the harbour should be flooded one day, but no one seemed concerned when the tides were high, as they were today, the sea almost running over onto the pavements on the quay. She mentioned it to Tommy as they made their way with Ronnie and Liz past the waxed bonnets of the cars parked up outside the Peninsula, but he just laughed and said she took her mother's folk tales too seriously.

'What tales are those?' Ronnie asked, raising his eyebrows, ready to be entertained, watching as Tommy held out a chair for Elsa before taking a seat himself.

'Gloomy Welsh myths, Ronnie boy,' Tommy said, opening his eyes wide, and they both laughed, and Tommy slapped his big hands against his thighs. Elsa loved Tommy's hands. She'd married him for them. A farmer's hands like shovels, with blunt-edged fingers, they reminded her of where she came from and what her people did, either farming the land, or travelling the world as merchant seamen or a little of both, as Tommy's family had always done. When she turned his hands over, she could trace the lines in his palms, as if they made a map of New Quay that she carried with her everywhere. When she took him to bed, he spoke to her in Welsh and ran his farmer's hands over her breasts. She remembered the day he asked her to marry him, the red round perfection of the sun on the water at Cwmtydu's deserted cove, and the gritty feel of sand in her underwear afterwards, and being glad that she wouldn't be considered a child any more, now that she had a fiancé.

Ronnie had drunk too much champagne already and was staring at her.

'Fabulous dress, Elsa,' he said.

Liz lit up a cigarette.

'Thank you, Ronnie.' Elsa bent over to kiss him on the cheek. 'Happy Birthday.'

'Thank you, honey.' He held onto her hand for longer than he should.

'Is your husband jolly already?' said Tommy to Liz, trying to catch the waiter's eye.

'He's been drinking all afternoon,' she answered, not smiling back.

'I see we have some catching up to do, Ronnie boy.' Tommy held his arm up in the air, shaking his big fingers instead of clicking them, and a young Chinese boy in a white, double-buttoned jacket appeared at their table, holding an empty silver tray against his stomach.

'A bottle of champagne,' Tommy said. 'No, make that two.'

The boy bowed. He turned the tray over and cleared the empty glasses from the table.

By the time they'd finished the second bottle of champagne, the marble floor had started to move around under Elsa's feet and she'd got used to the noise of the wind shaking the windows that opened out onto the front of the hotel.

'I need the ladies,' she mouthed to Liz.

'I'll come with you.' Liz reached for her bag.

In the restroom Elsa went straight into a cubicle to tidy up her dress. She heard the door outside open and close and Mimi Forsyth's voice say, 'You look nice, Liz.'

'Starting to fill out now.' Liz sounded happy again. 'Lively in here tonight, isn't it?' The words were distorted, as if she was frowning at herself in the glass as she applied another layer of lipstick.

'People are making the most of the good times, I suppose.'

The tiny stitches in Elsa's dress were jumping around in front of her eyes, but when she looked closely, they were as perfect and close-set as they had been in the Wangs' shop.

'Where's Elsa?' Mimi said.

Liz made a non-committal noise. She must still be at the mirror, applying swirls of lipstick the colour of candy.

'That dress,' said Mimi. 'Don't you think it makes her look a little… well, you know… as if she's…'

'Gone native?'

'You should talk to her.'

Liz's reply was lost as the door screeched open and shut. When Elsa came out of the cubicle, they were both gone. Her hands trembled as she washed and dried them. The red walls were crowding in on her, and all she could see were the dulled edges of the mirror frame above the sink where the gold leaf had flaked off. But when she looked at her reflection, she could see that the roundness in her face that used to make her look as if she was always smiling, or about to, had become more angular, more knowing, and there was a soft knuckling of bone across her shoulders.

In the long, windowless corridor running from the restrooms back to the stairs down to the lobby, the people who were walking towards the bathrooms avoided the gaze of those who had just left them. Elsa kept her eyes down too. Her mouth was dry and she had a headache. She wondered how long it would be before Tommy would be ready to go home.

'Mrs Jones?'

She looked up.

'Yes?'

She recognised him straightaway.

'It's Oscar, Oscar Campbell,' he said. He reached a hand out as if to shake hers but when she took it and leaned in to accept a kiss, he pulled back.

'How are you?'

No one had asked her how she was, not since that day at the hospital. Sometimes she hated good manners.

'I'm sorry,' he said. 'I didn't mean to upset you.'

'No, not at all. It's very kind of you to ask.'

'I was so very sorry about... your baby,' he said.

She realised he was still holding onto her hand and she wanted to cling onto it, this firm, truthful grip on her loss. She watched him as he tried to readjust the tenor of their conversation to something more in keeping with the social niceties people were supposed to exchange over drinks and dinner at the Peninsula.

'I'm surprised to see you still in Hong Kong,' he said.

'Why should you be surprised?'

'So many of the wives have left already. Gone home, or to Australia.'

'Oh, that,' she said, waving a hand, realising that her movements were exaggerated and that she really had drunk too much champagne. 'Tommy says it's nothing to worry about. It'll all blow over, he says. He knows a lot of journalists, and they keep him in the know.'

'Does he?' Oscar said. 'In any case, it's very good to see you.'

He seemed so stiff and formal that she couldn't help smiling as he moved off. He had a quick, long stride and within seconds he had disappeared around the corner.

She loitered at the top of the staircase. A string quartet was playing on one of the balconies. The lobby below seemed a long way away. People who were sitting at the tables in small groups had split up and joined different groups, or had their tables moved together to make one big one. Everyone was laughing and shouting to make themselves heard. Elsa listened to their voices, mainly English, but also French and Dutch in places, rise to the ceiling and mix into a noisy babel where she was standing.

She could see Ronnie still slumped back in his chair. Liz was sitting up straight, both hands on her handbag, as if she was ready to go.

Tommy's seat was empty.

She looked all around the lobby, at the sea of black dicky bows and evening dresses punctuated by the white jackets of the waiters.

There was a couple standing by a tall potted palm between the lobby and one of the corridors leading off it. If you were sitting down at one of the tables you would hardly know they were there, much less who they were. But Elsa knew Tommy's wide jaw, and his big hands. She knew the thick, flat fingers that were running their way down the back of Mimi Forsyth's dress before coming to rest on her behind. She knew how it felt to be pressed against him like that, feeling the rush of blood pulsing under her skin.

Groups of people in the lobby below were still swirling around, connecting into clumps of shifting colour: from up here they looked like a marked-out territory that was constantly changing. And then the wind battered against the windows again, so loudly that there was a hiatus in the noisy conversations below, and Elsa wondered if it would all turn to sea under her eyes, if this group of people would disappear under the water forever, somehow complicit in their own undoing. Just like the story her mother used to tell her when she was little, about the gatekeepers who got drunk and forgot to close the sea gates on the low-lying land of Cardigan Bay. The whole village was flooded while its inhabitants lay sleeping. Except when her mother told her the story, stroking her hair while the wind shook the windows in their sashes, she had felt safe.

Tommy said it was important for him to mix with the right people. That was what he had said when Elsa asked about Mimi.

She saw a shock of red hair moving through the crowd below. Oscar. It looked as if he was going from group to group, telling them something. People started to gather their belongings and make their way to the main doors.

Tommy and Mimi came back to the table where Liz and Ronnie were sitting. Ronnie had fallen asleep with his mouth open, and Tommy had to shake him to wake him up.

Elsa went down to the lobby and walked towards the table.

'Elsa, we have to go.' Tommy looked hot in his dinner jacket and he was speaking too quickly. 'There's a storm coming in.'

Elsa watched the water surge in a dark mass around them.

'What if we go under?' said Liz.

Elsa stared straight ahead at the lights of Victoria, thousands of them against the black sky. A cruiser passed by in a hurry, causing a sudden swell that lifted the *sampan* up like a buoy. She could hear Tommy next to her telling her to hold on tight. Mimi was sitting on the other side of him. She looked green.

'I think I'm pregnant again,' Elsa said to Tommy, half-shouting over the sound of rushing wind and water.

Tommy said something, but there was too much noise and Elsa couldn't catch what it was. Mimi put her head down, still clinging to the wooden back of the seat in front.

'I feel so ill,' she groaned.

'It's sea legs you need,' Elsa said under her breath.

6

Elsa didn't pass any of this on to Nannon when she wrote. Elsa told her the due date and sent her a list of the things she needed.

Something to look forward to! Nannon wrote back, underlined twice. *I'll be ticking off the weeks. Tommy must be thrilled.*

Elsa hadn't seen Tommy like this before, distant and hungover. When she'd first met him in New Quay, he'd been home on leave between postings, sitting at the kitchen table with his collar unfastened, eating all his favourite foods, which his mother Sara had made specially: *cawl*, home-baked bread, damson wine. When Elsa had walked in under the low beam of the door that led straight from the *buarth* into the kitchen, Sara was standing over him, arms folded across her chest, watching him eat. He'd glanced up with the soup spoon held halfway between the bowl and his mouth, and kept it there, looking at her as Sara came over to her, taking her coat and basket, and telling her to take a seat at the table. The bench had creaked as she'd sat down – Tommy had joked about that later on, how could the bench have protested under her weight, and her a bag of bones? – and by the time she'd got up from the table again, her stomach still warm from the *cawl*, it was understood that he would take her on a tour of the farm, although she'd been there many times to collect eggs while he'd been away at sea. They went to the milk shed to see the cows, and he told her about his work on the coast off mainland China, capturing pirates, confiscating contraband and taking it ashore. She'd listened while the tails of the cows slapped against their soft behinds, and looked away as the boy on the stool pressed their udders until milk squirted into the bucket at his feet. When Tommy said '*Hwyl*,' to him, the lad had kept one eye on the stream of warm milk as he tipped his cap at Elsa.

Tommy had said goodbye to her at the gate onto the road from Capel y Wig down to New Quay, the sharp edge of the wind giving him red cheeks.

In Hong Kong all the men were pale and languid, and on the mornings when Tommy didn't go into work until lunchtime he looked wan and listless too; he sat in the apartment in his dressing gown, reading the newspaper and eating a second breakfast. But this was what she had chosen, Elsa thought, watching the Bentley easing its way down the hill, and closing the door behind him. That's what Nannon had said to her the morning she and Tommy had got married at Llanina Church, which was so far out on the headland that the water had almost lapped at their ankles when they came out into the sunshine for their photographs. Nannon had been standing behind Elsa, fixing her hair for her, and she'd said that when you get married you don't just choose a man, you choose a life. Elsa had felt a flicker of irritation when she'd said that, playing the older, sensible sister. What was Nannon to know about marriage? She was nearly thirty and wasn't even engaged. It had been cold, and on the road back to New Quay for the reception at the Penwig the first primroses had winked their yellow eyes at her from the high hedges. Perhaps Nannon was right, though. She thought of Sara, who'd stood over the table that day at Pwllbach while she and Tommy had talked and eaten, watching them together, a satisfied look on her face.

Elsa missed Nannon. She missed having someone to talk to, someone to tell her the baby would be fine this time. She wiped her eyes on a clean handkerchief and went to put it in the laundry for Lam. She went back to the terrace and sat in her usual place, watching the sun moving from one end of the sky to the other, counting the days.

II

Lin:
HONG KONG, 1941

1

I arrived in Hong Kong at daybreak. I stood on deck and watched the sun split open over the harbour, spilling light like a silkworm pushing its way out of a cocoon.

I was taken to the port office with the other girls. People came to collect them, but no one came for me. There were two men sitting behind a desk, one in a black uniform with gold brocade at the cuffs, the other in a linen suit. The man in uniform took off his white peaked cap and put it down next to his notebook; each time he asked me a question in English, the man in linen started translating it into Cantonese straightaway, too quickly, each voice drowning out the other, and I could make neither head nor tail of what was being said. If you had been there with me, Third Sister, I might have smiled inside, but you were far away and I was nervous.

I'd had plenty of time to prepare my answers, sitting with the others, talking as the mountains glided by, until we got to the junction of the three rivers. No one knew then what would come next, and we were all quiet until we reached Victoria Harbour.

I showed the men my piece of paper, and told them I had a sponsor coming to meet me, but they didn't believe me.

'Where is she?' they asked.

That question I couldn't answer. Lam had said she would be here.

'Perhaps she hasn't yet finished work,' I said.

The man in uniform behind the desk laughed then, and lifted his pen, shaking drops of ink off the nib. It wasn't a nice laugh.

'What did he say?' I asked the Chinese man in the English suit.

He said, 'What is her job, that she is out walking the streets until dawn?'

'She is a *ta chup* in a rich household, and now they need an amah to look after the baby, and she has sent for me.'

They put me to sit on a bench in the corridor. While I waited, I watched the pieces of paper pinned to the cork board opposite flutter as people came in and out of the main door to the building, sending a hot draught of air up the stairwell. Each time the door opened, I could hear sounds from the harbour outside, crates being dragged down gangplanks, men's voices shouting instructions, the chugging of engines, and heavy coils of rope being flung onto the jetty. When it was closed I could be quiet in myself again, my thoughts accompanied only by the mechanical humming that filled the air around me: not dragonflies, nor Mother singing to herself as she walks out into the fields when she wakes, but the rhythmical whirring of a fan hanging from the ceiling.

They called me back into the office.

'We will have to make other arrangements,' they were saying, when Lam came into the room. She looked as if she had been in a rush to get here.

'*Mui mui*,' she said.

Her face was gleaming with sweat and her plait was coming loose. She was wearing a red *cheongsam* with a slit up the side, and lipstick. So this was what she looked like now she was a Hong Kong girl. Maybe soon I would look like this too. The English man glanced at me as if he was thinking the same thing.

'Your sister,' he said through the interpreter. First Sister, I wanted to add.

62

It was only once we were out on the street that Lam pulled me to her. She looked just as she always had, with a dimple to one side of her mouth when she smiled, but the expression in her eyes wasn't the same as before, not as bright and cheeky.

'It's my day off,' she said. 'I'll take you to the *kongsi fong* and then I have to go.'

'Where?' I said, but she pressed her shiny lips together and didn't answer.

I followed her. She hadn't offered to take one of my bags, and my arms were dragged down as I walked behind. There were men pulling rickshaws, and women standing at open stalls pointing at fish darting about in shallow containers filled with water. People were all around me, the rising heat of the day coming off them. It wouldn't have surprised me if I'd heard their hearts beating underneath their skin in time with the clip-clop of their clogs against the pavement. I saw men glancing at Lam as they passed us. She kept her head still and stared straight ahead, which only made them look again.

'Keep up,' she said to me.

I wanted to ask how far we had left to walk, but I was afraid to speak out loud, knowing that my accent would give me away to these strangers, that even the sound of my own voice would make me homesick.

'We're here,' she announced, turning round and taking one of the bags.

She waved her arm towards a door propped open by a bicycle between a fruit seller's and a laundry. The paint was peeling off the frame and the rush mat on the other side of the threshold was worn through.

'Home,' she said, smiling for the first time. 'Come on.'

I followed her, holding on tight to the handles of my bag. It was dark inside after the morning sunlight on the streets. There were walls all around, and air that had been inside for too long,

63

and no windows. I blinked a few times, to get the dust and tears out of my eyes, held out an arm to the banister, and pulled my way up the steps without giving myself time to think about going back.

Upstairs, there was a long window overlooking the street. The walls were covered with shelves loaded with bags like mine, clothes folded inside. Open-topped bamboo baskets were hooked up from the low ceiling. There were low, narrow cupboards of different shapes and sizes, all styles. They too were covered with objects: thermos flasks, bottles, and tins. Next to the door was a mirror with a wooden frame, surrounded by four small mirrors. There was a row of five beds against a far wall, each divided from the other by a partition made of poor wood, the kind that Father would sell to make a fire. They were slatted into bars, so that each bed had some light from the window as well as a small space all along one side and one end. There was an empty bed next to the window.

'This is yours,' Lam said, putting my bag down on the bare floor. I sat down on the bed and looked across to the building opposite, at a girl sitting on a bed next to an open window like mine, looking back at me. I breathed in the smell of shark's fin soup coming up from the street, and remembered the bed I grew up in, with all of us sleeping together, bound up tight in heavy blankets in winter, each other's sweat trickling along our limbs in summer, so familiar it felt like our own.

Lam moved away to her own bed, closest to the door, a good distance from the noise and smell of the street, and put her handbag down on it. She went to the mirror to comb and plait her hair.

'I'll do it,' I said.

She smiled again, but she looked as if she was thinking of something else.

'When will we go to work?' I asked, knotting her hair carefully so the plait was neat but not too tight.

'Not today.'

She turned to the side and patted her hair to make sure it was smooth where I'd combed it back from her face. 'It's my day off, I told you. Tomorrow morning, you will come with me, and help me until Mrs Elsa is awake and ready to see you. Now, get some rest. I have to go out for a while, but I'll bring you something to eat when I come back.'

I didn't ask her again where she was going. I sat back on my bed and looked down onto the street, at all the heads bobbing up and down, and at the corner of the harbour that I could see from here, through the steam coming up from the hawkers' stalls selling hot noodles. The water would have been beautiful in the sun if I had been able to see it, but it was covered in junks and tugs all driving at each other to see who could get past first, until a liner nosed its way through, forcing them back.

I thought of you, Third Sister, and my promise to write. I took a few cents from my purse and went down into the street. I was afraid, and wondered how I would find my way back. I hoped I wouldn't have to walk too far, and it must have been my day for good fortune after all, because I had only walked two blocks when I saw him, the letter-writer, with his stall set up on the pavement, a piece of canvas on two poles with scrawled-over pieces of paper tacked up behind him, and a small table across his knees. He saw me before I saw him. By the time I caught his eye he already had his hand held out to usher me to the stool that sat empty in front of him.

I sat down and words deserted me. I didn't know what to say, where to begin.

'Where have you come from?' he asked me gently, reaching for his pen. He had two pots on the table, one for brushes, one for pens. Sheaves of paper were rolled up underneath his chair, on a tray. He pulled out one of the smallest ones. He must be used to this. A girl off one of the ships from the Pearl River Delta, still smelling of the mulberries that grow on her parents' poor smallholding. He knew what to expect. A few words, just to let the family know I've arrived. You too will have to pay someone to read it to you, after all.

'Between Canton and Dongguan,' I whispered, the words catching in my throat despite my best intentions, and somehow, just saying the names attached to my birthplace brought my story out all in a rush, like the rivers that run downstream towards the South China Sea. Once I had begun I found it easy to keep going, and although I had only given him a little money, the letter-writer kept going too, until I saw that his knuckles had turned into swollen yellow bulbs like lychees, and he let the pen drop from his grip.

I picked it up from the pavement and put it on the table.

'I'm sorry,' I said getting up. 'It's just that there is so much to say.'

'Yes,' he said, handing me the letter in its envelope. 'Only a cent a time. Make sure you come back and see me again.' He smiled as he handed it to me.

I didn't tell him I wasn't even sure that I would find my way back to his stall again. To me the street signs and shop hoardings were meaningless scribbles, just like the letter I'd paid him to write. But I was sorry to leave. He had taken something of me and put it down on paper to keep always, and if I'd been able to read it, I wonder if I might have hung onto that letter for myself.

2

I don't know much yet, but the English words my new mistress uses are starting to take root, flowering into whole sentences about Mari's naps, her walks, and what clothes she should wear.

When Mari wakes up and has just been changed, she likes to have five minutes in my arms to come to, stretching her hands around her, feeling her way like a blind man, running her fingers over my cheeks and lips. I pretend to snap at her fingers, playing shadow puppets on the wall. She smiles for the first time, full of delight at herself for being able to show her pleasure. She reminds me of you, Third Sister, so calm and trusting. And holding her reminds me of myself at seven years old, sitting on the threshold, waiting for Mother and Father to come back from the fields, rocking you in a shawl our grandmother made years ago for First Sister, the winter after the bad summer that only our parents can remember. Mother always cried when she talked about that summer, although not in front of you.

After lunch, Mrs Elsa will call out from the living room, 'Ah Lin. Are you ready to take Mari out?'

'What?' I say. She speaks so quickly; sometimes it is difficult to follow what she is saying. It is a shame Captain Jones is hardly ever home. He speaks our language, because of his customs work. He tells me he learned it from the pirates he has to chase, although I don't think he is serious. He is funny, always joking, even if supper is running late or Lam has broken an ornament when she's been dusting, her mind on other things. 'It was only some old tat from Wan Chai market,' he will say, patting Mrs Elsa's arm, making her laugh too.

'Time for Mari's walk, dear,' she'll say again, coming into the nursery and stroking the top of Mari's head.

Mari's life is like a quartered orange, cut into segments of feed, wash, change, sleep. Looking after her is easy; when it is time for the next task, there is a shift in the air between us. She turns her head in the cot and gurgles at me, or waves her arms, as if she is trying to get up on her own, without help. Soon she gets stronger; when I feed her she puts out one hand, tapping rhythmically on the bottle as if she would like to feed herself. She keeps her eyes fixed on mine.

Today was different from our usual routine, although things started out as they always did. The road wound crookedly down the hill, making a shape against the Peak like a bonsai tree that I could see in miniature from Wan Chai on my days off. It seemed so far away, then, the apartment and the captain and Mrs Elsa. And Mari, waking up in her darkened room wondering where I was, I was sure, and crying for me, and me not coming because I always went back to the *kongsi fong* on the days I wasn't working, as I was supposed to.

I held on tightly to the curved steel handle of the pram, and pulled my weight away from it to stop it rolling too quickly down the hill. I was happy, because taking Mari for a walk for an hour or two was as good as a day off to me – no, better, because I was away from the apartment, and all the jobs I was supposed to do, one after the next, but I still had Mari with me. It was the middle of the afternoon and the air still quivered with heat. I adjusted the shade over Mari's face, keeping one hand firmly on the pram. There were mosquitoes hanging in clouds under the trees, and butterflies dancing black and orange among them. I turned the final corner, and made my way along a back street to the botanical gardens.

It was Lam who had sent me there first.

'All the girls from home go there,' she'd said.

'That sounds lively.'

'If you have nothing else to do, I suppose.'

Lam didn't seem to like anything any more, apart from her fortnightly holiday. She worked thirteen days in a row on the promise of a day off. She would begin her fortnight with her head down and her eyes bleary. She would find it difficult to smile, even at Mrs Elsa, and she didn't exchange two words with me. She never told me what she did or where she went; she just left her things at the *kongsi fong* and abandoned me there in the dingy half-light, and I didn't see her until she woke me the next morning for us to start our journey up to work for five. Sleepy myself, I would always forget to ask Lam about her day's holiday until we were at the apartment, standing straight in our clean white tunics and black lawn trousers, waiting for Mrs Elsa to come and inspect us and give us our instructions for the day. By then it would be too late, and the day's work would press in on us without restraint.

In the afternoons, though, everything would open up around me again as I made my way down the hill with the pram. The botanical gardens were filled with the sound of laughter. The spaces on the grass under the biggest trees were always taken by other girls dressed in black and white uniforms like me, and rows of perambulators parked in the shade to keep them cool. Crawling around on the grass with the water lilies spread out lazily in the shallow pond behind them were small white buds of babies – grouped together in some places, and spread out singly in others.

'Hello Lin,' said the girl next to me. She wore her plait rolled into a chignon on the back of her head and when she smiled she showed her full cheekbones.

We took our babies out of their prams and passed them round, each admiring the other's, as that was the polite thing to do.

'Celia has another tooth!' said one, holding up a stocky baby with blonde hair.

'My daughter has three – look!' said another. She is from Sam Sui. That is why she is always determined to better everyone else, Mother would say. 'My daughter' is what we all call our babies. Even though they're not our babies. We understand what is meant by it.

'My daughter is still too little for teeth,' I said, holding up Mari for inspection. I knew it didn't matter that Mari had nothing to show yet – no teeth, no funny crawl on her bottom, no first words, in Cantonese or English. My daughter has the prettiest eyes and the sweetest disposition. She never cries.

We put our babies back in their prams and started to leave the park in twos and threes. When I looked back there was no one left apart from a tired coolie who had taken our place on the bench in the shade. He had a shaved head and wore nothing but a pair of shorts; across his back you could see where sweat mixed with fish salt had dried on his skin. He was eating rice from a bowl, holding it up with one hand to catch every grain, his head tilted right back.

I waited at the gates for Wang. I hoped that I wasn't late. I had forgotten to ask one of the others if it was four o'clock yet, and I knew Mrs Elsa would need help to get ready to go out for dinner. I had kept Mari out of the pram and strapped her to my back to carry her the length of the park. I sang to her as we waited. She chuckled in my ear, then fell asleep, her breathing slowing and deepening, resting her head against the back of my neck.

I was about to take her out of the straps and put her in the pram when Wang pulled up in the car. He parked up close to the kerb, ready to lift the pram straight into the boot without trouble. Mrs Elsa was sitting in the back. She moved over towards me as I loosened the ties, her hands held out ready to take Mari. I sat back against the leather seat.

'I hope I'm not late, Mrs Jones,' I said.

'No, not at all, Ah Lin.' She held Mari close to her in her lap. She wasn't smiling the way she usually did. 'I'm not going out now, in any case.'

'Poor you. Poor Mr Tommy.' I wished I had more English. I didn't like having to search for the right words.

'Oh, Mr Tommy's still going out,' she said. 'It's just me that's staying at home.'

I should have been enjoying my ride in this grand car, but the seat was slippery and Ah Wang drove too fast. And I didn't like Mrs Elsa's sad expression. It made me feel as if I didn't know what to do next.

We were just about to turn onto our cul-de-sac when I saw Lam, walking with a man. A white man, in a soldier's uniform. The smile on her face made her seem like a young girl again. I glanced over at Mrs Elsa, but she was looking at Mari, stroking the single strands of hair on her forehead.

I could see Wang's eyes in the mirror. He looked angry. He banged the double doors to the garage as he put the car away.

'She's playing a dangerous game,' he said to me, sitting over his tea in the kitchen. 'If they see her with him that will be the end of things for all of us. They'll think we're not to be trusted.'

When we got back I had nothing to do. Mrs Elsa said she would look after Mari until bedtime. She went into the living room and closed the door, and I clacked my way up and down the passage like an abandoned mah-jong tile.

I went into the kitchen and stood next to Lam while she washed up. She told me the man's name was Ryan. He drank Mexican beer and had deep pockets. He was a Canadian soldier. Mrs Elsa and the captain spent all their time chasing happiness, didn't they, Lam said to me, so why not us? I didn't have the heart to disagree with her.

She soaped and rinsed the plates with absent-minded strokes, staring out of the window, dreaming of a long voyage on a steam ship to Canada, a house to call her own, and a life far away from this one.

3

It was just a practice, the air-raid siren. A dummy run, the captain called it. I liked the way he said it, nice and gentle, reassuring. We were supposed to carry on as usual.

The papers hanging off newsstands ran big headlines alongside photographs of the new air-raid shelters they've put up downtown. It looked like a scene from a street opera: wardens in uniform stood in a line while a crowd of Wan Chai shoppers looked on open-mouthed. Above the low concrete blocks, which had 500 PERSONS daubed on them in oily paint, were hoardings pasted with man-sized advertisements for soft drinks and flower cakes. There must have been at least five hundred people right there on the street. A hawker had set up shop at the head of the crowd, facing away from the shelter, selling produce directly from her basket.

I wanted to buy the newspaper to show the letter-writer the next time I saw him, so he could read me the story that went with the picture, but I had just posted what was left of my month's wages home, sending everything I had left because of Mother's cough.

I walked around in a daze. Mari had just started teething and I was getting no sleep. She would be settled down as usual, but after an hour or so she would scream loudly out of the blue; the noise would slice into my dreams like the air-raid sirens, waking me instantly. At first I didn't know what to do, what could be wrong, so I stood helplessly over her cot and watched her cry, as she wouldn't let me touch her. When I realised what it might be, I rubbed poppy syrup into her gums to soothe them, feeling the enamel of her milk teeth about to push through the skin, hard against my fingers. I washed and changed her and gave her a fresh nappy. Then we would sit in the nursing chair by the window for a while watching gunboats passing up the channel under the low moon; I would put a few drops of gripe water on the tip of a teaspoon and get Mari to swallow them, and then, once she had calmed down, I'd put her back to sleep. She was over nine months old by this time though, with teeth coming through one after the other. When she had been through a bad week, I would sigh with relief to see the sharp tip of a tooth poking out of the bloody gum like a tiny white fin, only to be woken a few nights later by the next one. I got used to it. I got up and applied the necessary treatments all in the same order each time without thinking. When it was over I fell back to sleep, only to be woken after two hours to go through the whole thing again. In the mornings we slept late and woke up with our eyes dry and itchy: it was as if Mari and I had been on a long journey through dreams peopled with vague grey shapes that moved silently past us, alone with each other. I think she felt it too. She pulled in close to me, holding onto the ends of my hair. 'Ta-da, Ta-da, Ta-da,' she said, over and over. 'Shhh!' I said to her, giggling, because it was a joke between Mrs Elsa and the captain that Mari had decided she was only going to say one word, for the moment at least, and that word was going to be something that sounded like 'Daddy'.

I no longer spent my days off in the *kongsi fong* looking out of the window; instead I walked around Victoria and Central and Sheung Wan, breathing in as much cool air as I could. It wasn't always clean air, especially if I was walking along the waterfront, past the ferry terminal and the cargo jetties, but it felt fresh after the long nights in Mari's nursery. I told myself I didn't want company, but I went to see the letter-writer more and more, just to talk. He seemed to understand that I didn't need him to talk back, and I began to spend longer at his stall. I enjoyed the open, honest expression on his face, and the peaceful scraping sound that his pen made on the paper. When the letter was finished and folded away in its envelope, he would take his glasses off and rub the inner corners of his eyes with his forefinger and thumb. Then he would sit back with his hands clasped in his lap.

Today, though, he kept his hands on the table. His fingers weren't touching mine, but as he looked at me, I wondered what it might feel like if they were, if this was how Lam felt when she was with Ryan.

He pointed up at one of his signs, hung up alongside the calendars and illuminated scripts.

'You see that saying up there?'

I nodded, although of course both he and I knew it meant nothing to me.

'To Choose A Lucky Day,' he said. 'I hadn't intended on working on the day you came to me first. But then a feeling came over me that this was going to be a special day, and that I must work, even though I was tired. So I came and set up stall as usual. I hung up my work as you see it now, unfolded my table, set out the stools, took four small bricks and put them under the table legs so it wouldn't wobble as I wrote. I did everything exactly as I always do it. And then something happened. You arrived. And I realised that I had indeed chosen my lucky day, Lin.'

But I didn't know what to say. I still felt it, that unfurling inside me, as I watched his still face, with one eyelid that hung down just a little lower than the other, and I wanted him to keep on looking at me across the table that didn't shake on its legs, but I was thinking of the spring day when I came to Hong Kong. I had left Canton to make money for you, that's the truth, but also to see something other than the relentless furrows of our fields, the tireless wriggling of the silkworms, more demanding than babies. I wanted to get away, and have no one to think about but myself, once my money was safely on its way to you every month. I wanted to sit in the botanical gardens in the company of friends, with showers of water spraying out of hoses in the background. I wanted to look at the beautiful clothes of women like Mrs Elsa, and to care for a baby like Mari, who has everything already, so all I have to give her is love. I had never thought about a man before I left Canton, except Father, and when I left I was glad not to have to think about him any more.

'Would you like me to teach you to write your name, Lin?' the letter-writer said. 'And then,' he whispered, putting the tips of his fingers very lightly on my nails, 'I can teach you how to write mine.'

The stool screeched against the pavement as I got to my feet. I walked quickly the way I had come, back to the *kongsi fong*. I didn't look back. I didn't want to see his puzzled face.

The streets were quieter than I had ever seen them; shops were closed and doors to buildings usually kept open were securely barred. Washing, hung to dry on ropes that ran above the street from one building to the block opposite, flapped in the breeze like paper birds. In the *kongsi fong* my feet made an empty sound against the wooden stairs, as if there was no one else in the building, and when I got to our room I saw that some of the other girls had cleared out their belongings and gone. I sat in my cubicle and surveyed the contents of my life: three bags of clothes and a bottle of lavender water that Mrs Elsa had given me. I thought to myself, even if I wanted to go home now, where would that be – the Pearl River Delta,

Sheung Wan, the Peak? There's a little of me that has been scattered through them all and taken root there, and to try to cut the shoots that have pushed their way out like sweet potato leaves and bring them together in one harvest would make me someone else entirely. Whoever that person would be, she wouldn't be me.

4

I was up on the roof terrace hanging out the washing when the bombing started. Although I had wrung the sheets out by winding them tight, they were still heavy with water and awkward to pull up onto the line without letting the other end drag on the dusty tiles underfoot. The early morning sky was misty above Victoria, and over in Kowloon the rows of windows along the wharf glinted in the sun. At the bottom of the hill was the race course, the grass cut so short it looked like a green lake. I was happy, although it was cool and I had come up without a coat, and hanging wet sheets was always hard work. I enjoyed the peace of these few moments on the terrace alone, when I could think about the rest of the day, about what Mari was going to wear, when we would go to the park, and the noodles and fresh fruit Lam and I had bought for our supper.

The first thing I heard was the drone of aeroplanes from the other side of the hill. I turned round to look, but my hands were full of damp linen so I couldn't shade my eyes and had to scrunch them up against the sun. Flying in over the Peak like squat, gorged mosquitoes were six planes, so low I could see the burning red circles painted on their sides. As they flew over the apartment their undercarriages started to open. They must have been about halfway down the hill when they released their load. The first bomb fell on the cemetery on Ko Chiu Road, and the earth opened up like a flower, sending out

78

a shower-burst of chipped slabs, metal vases, bits of wood and incense sticks.

After that there was another boom, and another, more smoke and debris floating up through the wooded hill that separated us from the rest of the city. I ran down the steps from the roof, through the apartment to the living room, pegs snapping against the linoleum as they scattered all around me, a bundle of washing still in my arms.

There was no one there. The captain had gone to the customs office early. It was Christmas morning, and he needed to deal with some urgent business before the festivities began, he'd said.

There were more hammering bangs – not from outside this time, but from inside, then the wrenching, splintering noise of doors being broken in. Down on the ground floor, then the second floor, then the apartment next door.

I ran to Mrs Elsa's dressing room, where she was sitting at her mirror doing her hair. She was still in her negligee, covered up by a house coat wrapped around her middle with one of her elegant sashes. She hadn't done her make-up and her face looked young.

'Hide!' she said straightaway. 'Hide Mari.' There was fear in her voice but no hesitation.

I went to the nursery and lifted Mari from her cot without my usual clucking and shushing and took her straight to the laundry room. The brass locks on the front door of our apartment were strong, and by the time the door had been kicked in I was crouched over in the empty clothes basket with Mari in my arms. I slotted the lid into place over our heads and hoped she wouldn't wake after being lifted so suddenly from her cot. I heard the back door of the apartment being pulled to, and thought that Lam and Wang must have decided to risk going the back way down to the garage, to hide in the Bentley's generous boot.

The laundry basket was made of wicker, with tiny slats all the way round. I sat and waited. There were men inside the apartment now. There were shouts, and the sound of heavy boots along the passageway, I didn't know how many pairs, maybe four or five. I heard someone kicking doors open in turn: the captain and Mrs Elsa's bedroom, Lam's tiny room. Mine. Wang's. The laundry room.

A pair of green canvas trousers came in, stopping next to the basket. I could smell sweat, men's sweat, bodies that needed washing. Every time I breathed, the darkened inside of the basket jumped and shook around me, like a volcano about to explode. I thought of the worst thing they might do. I remembered Mother's story about the Japanese soldier who liked to take the babies of his enemies, throw them in the air and watch them land on his raised sword, for fun. The victor's pleasure.

The green trousers were so close to me that I could see the bumps and shapes made by the textured khaki, craters and hollows forming and re-forming as he took each step towards the middle of the room. His view must have been obscured by some of the towels hung up to dry from a pulley; I heard him tut as he pushed them aside.

Mari opened one of her small fists in her sleep. Her fingers stretched out one by one. She grabbed onto my plait and pulled it like a horse's tail, her eyes still shut. I sank my teeth into my tongue to bury the pain.

The soldier had turned around and was making his way out of the room, pushing towels aside as he went.

They kicked the kitchen door open. I heard glass breaking, plates being thrown to the floor. Mari turned her head towards me in her sleep. I stroked her cheek with trembling fingers. She took a deep breath and settled back into her dreams again.

They were walking around the living room now, the sound of their boots muffled by the rug. Springs creaked as they sat down in the easy chairs. There was a tinkle of glasses.

I peeped out through the gaps in the laundry basket at the empty corridor. It looked as it always did. Framed photographs of the captain and Mrs Elsa hung on the wall, people dressed in winter coats standing on a beach next to a stormy sea, smiling at the camera. On the hall table was a black porcelain jug with inlaid flowers in gold lacquer. Next to it was an ornate clock.

I closed my eyes and willed this to be a normal day. The kind of day when everything would turn out exactly as I had planned it; the laundry, Mari's walk in the park, the pleasure of her nap-time before supper, when all I had to do was stay with her and let my thoughts wander. Mrs Elsa would be in the dressing room, while the captain sat out on the terrace enjoying a pink gin before dinner. I waited to hear the clink of ice cubes, the door to the sitting room opening and closing, and the silence of them kissing, before he served her a soda with lime, the way she has it every day when he comes home from work.

But when the sitting room door was opened again, the heels that tramped their way back out were even heavier than before, and unsteady. I don't know if it was the whisky that had reminded them what it was they were here to do, that time was not to be wasted. The dressing room door was kicked open. There was a click. A shot was fired.

Mrs Elsa didn't scream or shout. There were noises: cupboard doors being opened, or kicked in.

Mari was awake now, her eyes unblinking, staring at me in the dark. She didn't make a sound. The crown of her head smelled of sugar cane.

The door to the dressing room was flung open, and they came out again, the heavy boots. Their canvas trousers passed the laundry room door, which was still open. In the middle of them was Mrs Elsa, walking in her bare feet. I saw the lace trim bottom of her night gown. As they passed the hall table one of the men lifted an arm and casually pushed the porcelain jug. I heard the smash as it hit the floor.

The same thing had happened in the apartments all around us. People were being rounded up and herded out of the building. The soldiers shouted all the time, either at their prisoners or at each other, or both. I heard an engine outside, a lorry, or a truck.

One of them yelled in English: 'In! Get in!'

There was the crack of something hard against flesh and bone, a man's cry. Perhaps he hadn't moved quickly enough. They must all have been moving quickly after that, because I didn't hear it again. Doors were shut, a tailgate lifted and bolted into place. The engine chugged some more, shifted gear and moved off down the hill. Other trucks followed it, their tyres crunching through the wreckage from the blown-out cemetery.

Mari had fallen back to sleep. I kept on staring at the broken-up jigsaw view of the hallway from inside our cocoon. The thousand pieces of the shattered porcelain on the linoleum; the photographs on the wall above. There was one of Mrs Elsa and the captain standing in a field with a man and woman with white hair. Even though the picture was black and white, you could tell that the plants billowing out in the wind around them had grown from rapeseed. The flowers were so full and ripe they had blurred into one velvet cloud under the glass. Father would have been proud of such a good crop. No wonder the white-haired man was grinning, his hand on the belly of a tractor. Mrs Elsa looked taller than the rest of them, as if she had been cut out of a magazine and glued onto the picture.

I wasn't afraid any more. The men had gone.

My arms and legs were stiff from being curled up in the laundry basket with Mari. I limped straight into Mrs Elsa's dressing room. Her clothes had been pulled out of closets and armoires and ripped apart or thrown to the floor and stamped on under their dirty boots. Her plum-coloured silk evening gown had been cut open down the middle. A white chiffon dress had mud on the tunic. Printed blouses had been torn off their hangers and thrown all over the room, as if the men had been looking for something.

I went over to the dressing table. Mrs Elsa's jewellery box was open. She didn't wear much jewellery: 'You can't take it with you, can you?' was one of her favourite phrases. It was what she always said when Lam was helping her to get ready for a dinner at the Peninsula, or cocktails at the Gloucester. Lam said it meant there was no point spending big money on small items you'll have to leave behind when you die. But Mrs Elsa was proud of her gold-and-diamond watch, and her engagement ring, a ruby set into a band that she said was made of something called Welsh gold. It was so pale that it had looked almost silver against the black velvet of the box. It wasn't there now. The box was empty.

Remember the studio photograph Lam and I sent home to you, Third Sister, how you admired our black-and-white uniforms? You were awed by the fake flowers in vases that stood on a column between us, and the painted curtain that set the scene behind, the oily glimmer of the moon on the bark of a goat-horn tree. But it was our jewels you were most proud of, wasn't it? We both wore identical rings, and a bracelet on one arm, mine on my right, and Lam's on her left. Well, let me tell you a secret. Those jewels weren't paid for by Mrs Elsa and the captain. They weren't given to us in return for our hard work. They were painted on by the photographer's assistant. All the girls pay a few cents extra to have it done.

One of Mrs Elsa's pots of face cream had been left with its lid off. I put it back on so the flies wouldn't get to it.

Mari started to cry then. It was time for her breakfast porridge and milk. I looked up at the mirror. There was a hole in the middle of it the size of a coin where the bullet must have hit it. I saw a confused face broken up into shards that ran from the centre to the edges of the kidney-shaped glass: an eye here, a cheekbone there. It took me a moment to recognise it as mine.

Footsteps, light and hesitant, were coming up the stairs from the lobby. Lam and Wang. I picked my way through the piles of clothes and stood in the hall and waited for them. Mari was howling.

On the wall the clock was still ticking. It was eight o'clock.

5

The bombing had stopped, although clouds of black smoke still hung low over the mountains on the other side of Kowloon.

Wang drove down from the Peak, his head lowered as if he expected sniper fire, with Lam and me in the back. It could have been any other morning, with French doors opened onto terraces and tables set for breakfast, but there were chairs that had been pushed back, fine bone china cups knocked out of their saucers, and shattered windows. And it was so quiet, quieter even than the early mornings on the Delta, with the paddy fields opening out in all directions, when they have been flooded and the mud levelled and all that needs to be done is to plant the spiky young plants and wait for them to push their way out of the earth and turn yellow. Even you, Third Sister, young as you are, know that once a finger of red stains the fields, it is time to harvest the ripened grains.

'It won't take long to get to the customs office,' Wang said. 'The captain will know what to do.'

Two military vans came round the corner, and drove straight at us on the wrong side of the road. A Japanese soldier up front cocked his bayonet at Wang and gestured that he should pull over. Sweat prickled out of Wang's skin, running down the back of his neck, but by the time he'd parked, the vans were gone.

'We'd better get out of the car,' he said.

We walked the rest of the way to Central. There were other people doing the same thing, not looking at each other, hurrying.

When we arrived at the customs building, the door was bolted and there were two young men in their shirt sleeves on the pavement outside running lengths of adhesive strip across the windows.

'Please, Sir, where is everyone? Where've they gone?' Wang said.

One of the young men bit off a strip of tape between his teeth before replying.

'Building's closed.'

The other one pointed to the Hong Kong and Shanghai Bank building and some of the big hotels on the other side of the road.

In the Hong Kong Hotel people were sitting around the lobby in their good coats. Some of them had cases. A tall, thin waiter, his collar greying at the tips, was serving drinks from the bar. Behind him, a small boy was kneeling down, rolling a single pram wheel back and fore across the lobby using a stick. A couple of people looked up as we walked in, but that was all. I had thought I would recognise more of the faces, but the only person I knew was one of the captain's colleagues, Mr Vernon.

'Please Madam,' I said, going over to his wife. Her face was like a flat, clean plate, without any expression. She was holding a toddler on her knee, who wriggled about in her lap like a basket of eels. Mrs Elsa called her Lizzie – 'my good friend, Liz,' she said when she was talking about her to other people, but she didn't recognise me, or Mari, who was strapped onto my back, with her head close in to my neck. All you could see were the dark tufts of hair sticking out like paddy seedlings at the back. She could have been any baby.

'Please can you tell me where Captain Jones is?' I asked, and then, when she didn't reply, 'we are looking for Captain Tommy Jones. Japanese soldiers broke into the apartment this morning and took Mrs Jones away.'

She jumped up and screamed, then started to cry, hysterical.

Mr Vernon got up and shouted, 'For God's sake, she's terrified enough as it is, can't you see?'

Everyone in the lobby stopped talking and stared at us. The little boy's wheel rolled along the floor, the rubber hum of its tyre cutting through the quiet; then it hit the waxed panelling of the reception desk, and bounced away, back on itself.

'Just quit messing around, will you?'

I had never heard Mr Vernon sound so angry before.

The boy stopped short.

'Yes, Sir,' he whispered.

He crept towards the pillar where the wheel had come to rest, picked it up, and walked away on tiptoe.

Wang, who had been looking about the lobby, beckoned for Lam and I to follow him through to the covered walkway that led directly to the Gloucester, but there were hundreds of Chinese jammed in it end to end and there was no way for us to get through. They were sitting on the floor, talking quickly over each other's heads, passing things to each other – blankets, rice bowls, paper packages of food.

Wang pressed his way into the crowd and spoke to a man with a beard of fine white hair. After a few minutes he came back to where we were waiting.

'Dragon Arcade has been bombed,' he said. 'They're still taking the bodies away.'

Dragon Arcade is just off Des Voeux Road, exactly where my letter-writer sits, seven days a week, hoping for passing trade. There hasn't been a day that I've gone looking for him that he hasn't been there.

As we made our way back out of the lobby, a young man in a jacket who had been sitting with the Vernons came up to us. He looked like an office boy.

'Captain Jones is at the harbour office. He went to try to get tickets for the next passage out. But we've just heard that they've stopped the ships.'

'Thank you, Sir,' Wang said.

We went back to the car, but someone else had got to it first. One of the wing mirrors had been ripped off and the other one shot at. The windscreen had shattered. The smell of urine hung in the air, and when Wang opened the door on the driver's side and put his head in, he brought it out again straightaway, his hand covering his nose and mouth. I looked through the window and saw the brown smears that covered the cream leather, the flies that had gathered already.

You'd imagine that we would have been panicking and scared, wouldn't you? Not just walking along Jubilee Street, as if we were going to market for Mrs Elsa. But the truth is that we didn't know where to go or what to do and so we were just following our usual route through Sheung Wan back to the *kongsi fong*. I knew that Lam would want to collect her things. She had a ring that Ryan had given her, along with a red packet holding money. They really were going to get married, you see; Ryan was going to prove himself. Lam was sobbing as she walked behind me.

And then, with a rush as sudden as a click of the fingers, the streets were full again. Outside a fishmonger's, a man was desperately trying to push trolleys of skinned fish back inside, and to draw the metal shutters across, but he was surrounded by people helping themselves without paying. Wang shoved his way through to help. We followed him, but got caught up in the crowd. I felt them all around us, arms, elbows, hands, jostling and grabbing at what they could – white fish, crocodiles' tails, dried prawns – and making off with their overloaded baskets and panniers. I heard Lam's voice behind me, but there were people all around us now, moving off in haste once they'd taken what they could, and we were carried with them almost to the intersection with Bonham Road. Then I felt a hand in mine and Lam pulled me back into an empty doorway. The chaos around us continued: feet on pavements, voices close up to us shouting almost in my ear. A thickset man carrying a long stave and a smaller man with an axe in his hand came up to us and demanded our pocket books without delay. They weren't Japanese. They weren't soldiers. I knew one of them: the one with the axe owned the spice shop across the road from the *kongsi fong*. Every time he came out to shake out his shallow spice pan at the end of the day he used to look up at the sky before shutting up shop. It was him. There was no mistake. I was so shocked that I couldn't get my fingers to work quickly enough to bring my purse out and they shouted again, and the spice-seller grabbed the front of my tunic and tore it open. I stayed quiet, terrified they would spot Mari's blue eyes peeping out over my shoulder, although the shame I felt as they looked at my bodice hanging through the ripped tunic felt worse than anything I had ever felt before.

'Hold on to me.'

It was Wang. The thugs disappeared back into the mob. We went out onto the street again. I used one hand to hold the front of my tunic together as best I could. There was a high-pitched whine in the air and an explosion somewhere up the hill, and the putter of some kind of gunfire. Wang pushed against the backs and shoulders in front of us. People shouted and tried to push back, but we got through. We saw why this street was clearer than the others: there were bodies all over the road. There was one woman lying on her back with part of her stomach blown away. Her flesh was the violent red colour of ripe tomatoes cut open and turned inside-out. I tried to look away but I couldn't. Her face was still intact, perfect, apart from a large mole that protruded over her top lip. Lying next to her was a boy, three or four years old, his hand in hers. He was dead too. I don't know why I thought of Father, then, instead of Mother. It was always Mother who held my hand and showed me things, told me stories when I was a young girl. Not Father. He was always tired and grumpy, telling us we weren't working hard enough. My stomach was turning over, pushing my breath up into my chest.

As we turned back up the hill, I saw the letter-writer coming towards us, carrying his leather suitcase.

'Wei!' I knew his name, just as well as he knew mine.

'Lin,' he said, but his voice was swallowed up by the sound of an air-raid siren, so loud that it felt it was coming at us through the ground. Dust had settled into his hair and in the creases around his eyes, making him looked old. I put a hand out and held onto his forearm.

We passed an abandoned tea shop. Tea sets had been shot at, and a crate of bamboo handles had spilled across the pavement. Tins were buckled and peppered with bullet holes.

Wang came to a halt outside his parents' shop, and called out, 'Mother! Father!'

Someone pulled the shutter with its ornate top back a little way, and a head popped out. His mother.

'Quick, come inside,' she said to us.

Two portly English men in suits carrying briefcases were standing in a doorway on the other side of the street.

'Come,' she called over to them, and they ran across the street.

We all went down to the tiny cellar. It smelled damp and cold. No one spoke. We sat side by side. Lam had stopped crying. One of the English men had a newspaper folded on his lap. He saw me looking at it and passed it over.

At first I thought the shapes jogging up and down under the headline's fuzzy newsprint would disappear when I blinked, but they didn't. In the photograph men on horseback were riding through Central. Men in uniforms, with moustaches. Another group followed on behind. There was one man out front on his own, wearing white gloves, his right hand raised in a victory salute.

The soldiers were all Japanese. There was no one in the picture who wasn't Japanese.

We sat listening to the sound of each other's breathing. Wei took the newspaper out of my lap.

'What does it say?'

He read quickly, translating as he went along:

ENEMY ALIENS TO REPORT TO MURRAY PARADE GROUND
The Japanese military have sent out an order for enemy aliens to gather at Murray Parade Ground at 9.00 am on Monday 5th January, 1942. All passports must be presented. Further details will be released shortly.

'Who are the enemy aliens?' I said.

'Us?' Lam asked the English men.

'No,' said the one who had given us the newspaper. 'It means us.'

6

We had no nappies for Mari, no powdered milk, and no clean clothes for any of us. Lam said the best thing would be for us all to go to the *kongsi fong* to shelter, and Wang and Wei could go out after dark to try to find something to eat.

But as we turned the corner of Wing Lok Street, we saw there were roadblocks barring the way, and a Japanese soldier carrying a bayonet. When he saw us approaching, he took the gun down from his shoulder and held it with both hands, pointing at the ground.

'Yes?' he said.

'We need to get through,' Wei said.

'You can't.'

'Why not?'

'We are keeping the British here for now.'

We looked up at the windows above the closed shops. There were no hawkers on the pavement, and the lines that hung over the street from building to building were empty of washing. But there were pale faces at the windows, peering out through the dust and grime that covered the glass.

There were Japanese flags everywhere, on government buildings, banks and hotels. They were tied to the ferries that were still running, carrying the conquering army and their mules over from Kowloon. All along the waterfront we saw soldiers landing and unloading crates and trunks like any weekday docker, and no one trying to stop them, and on every street corner we saw a red-on-white circle of sun rising into the sky.

Wang said we should go back to the apartment to find what food and drink we could. If the prisoners were to gather on Murray Parade Ground in a few days' time, our *kongsi fong* would be vacated soon enough. We should hide in the apartment until the British were herded to the parade ground, he said. Lam gulped back another sob as she listened to us talking. Ryan's ring and money would be long gone by then.

There were more roadblocks, with people clustered around them like moths' eggs. One soldier, instead of answering a man's halting questions, gave him a jiu-jitsu kick in the face. The rest of the group scattered quickly.

We doubled back on ourselves and headed back to the Peak. The first British soldier we saw was a dead body hanging out of the window of a car. His face was upside-down but you could still see the surprised look in his pale eyes. The air around him smelled bad.

Mari was heavy on my back as we walked up the hill. She was awake, and bored, and kept beating against my shoulders with her sticky fists, and pulling my hair. I knew she was hungry, but every time she tugged at my plait it made me want to cry.

'Do you want me to take her?' Wei said.

'It's all right,' I said. 'We're nearly there now.'

We turned round and looked back over the water. A cruiser had been torpedoed and was leaning on its side. The city was pockmarked with gaps where bombs and shells had fallen.

In the cul-de-sac leading to the apartment block there were reddened footprints on sandstone, broken walls with chunks gouged out of them by grenades, even a bloodied khaki shirt, but the apartment itself was as we'd left it.

Once we were safe inside Wang boarded up the front door

with scraps of wood from the garage. Lam went to the kitchen to look for tinned food and dried milk, taking Mari with her.

I went to Mrs Elsa's dressing room. I pulled down three cases from the top of the big wardrobe with the inlaid walnut panels: one for Mrs Elsa, one for the captain, and one for Mari. I put a good quality woollen blanket at the bottom of the cases even though they took up a lot of room, then I packed each bag, rolling up sports dresses, plain coats and jackets, jumpers and slacks. For Mari I packed romper suits and a worsted knit jacket, a crochet sweater and one of her peek-a-boo bonnets.

I had to call Wei to sit on the cases to get them shut.

'Won't they be too heavy?' Wei asked.

'The captain can take some things out if he wants,' I said. I was trying not to think about the ship we could see down in the harbour – almost under water, with a hole bored through its middle by a Japanese torpedo. I tried not to think about the captain rushing to the ticket office, certain he was doing the right thing, getting a safe passage home for the three of them before the fighting got any worse. I knew that once he had decided what he was going to do he wouldn't have turned back. He would have gone all the way to the harbourmaster's office, queued up with the others, waited his turn, not given up, not taken no for an answer.

That night we closed the doors onto the verandah because it was cold. We could have sat in the sitting room to eat but we went into the kitchen, where it was warmer, and sat around the table. Wang said it would be too dangerous even to light a candle, and there was no point in letting people know we were there. As the darkness settled in folds around us, we talked and talked. I sat opposite Wei, listening to him speak about his aunt, how she had taken him in after his mother died, how growing up as a poor child in Hong Kong hadn't been so bad after all.

Lam started to tell him about our childhood, our work on the farm, the bare facts of our existence.

He nodded, listening carefully as if he had heard none of it before. I sensed him glancing over at me. I wondered how much of all the stories I've told him since I came to Hong Kong I've forgotten myself in the daily rush just to get by. His silhouetted face showed me that he had forgotten nothing. You, Third Sister, and Mother and Father all live even more vividly in his imagination now than you ever have in real life. I don't remember when you last wrote to me. Is Mother still coughing? Are you even still on the farm, Third Sister, or have you managed at last to run away to Canton after trying so many times? You were always so fixed on going your own way, to meet the world before you were ready. I was so afraid for you, watching as Father dragged you back to the farm by your plait. But maybe working in a sweet shop in Canton wasn't so dangerous a proposition for a young girl after all. Perhaps the most dangerous place for you was home, always within reach of the back of Father's hand.

Were any of us ever happy? I can still see myself lying underneath the thick leaves of a longan tree, cracking open the fruit shells and letting the juicy insides burst open in my mouth and feeling something like contentment. But then I left to follow Lam, and on that day when I sailed downriver to Hong Kong I felt myself splitting into two, me then and me now, and I've been caught between the two ever since. Wei is the only person who can bridge the gap. He is the person who gives me life.

That night, when we lay down next to each other on sheets that still smelled of Mrs Elsa, it was me who pulled him towards me, who pressed my fingers into the soft skin on his buttocks that had never seen the sun and squeezed them as he came inside me.

I got up in the middle of the night because Mari cried out from the nursery. When I came back Wei had fallen asleep on his stomach, with one arm outstretched, his hand fanned out over the empty space where I'd been lying. I moved it gently, lay down again, and fell straight back to sleep.

7

It was a clear morning. The streets around the parade ground were empty, apart from a single delivery man with hunched shoulders and bent legs pulling a trailer loaded with fish buckets. The azalea bushes leading up to the entrance greeted us harshly, their petals closed one minute and open the next, like a beggar pushing out cupped hands and refusing to take no for an answer.

The parade ground was covered with people from end to end. They looked as if they had been bleached of colour overnight. Everything about them seemed unfinished. There were women wearing coats without belts, and men in shirts that didn't do up. Hair that was normally oiled back sprung away from foreheads, and painted-on lips that usually pouted their way in and out of conversations had faded back into thin, pale lines on their owners' faces.

Some people had bags, or blankets that were being used as bags, tied clumsily and held together anyhow. Some were empty-handed, and they were the ones I felt the most pity for. Their hands hung at their sides, making their shoulders stoop and pulling all their features to the ground too. Some of the men had bruises and cuts to the face.

It was the women who were talking to each other, not the men. Hundreds of female voices rose up into the air with a shrill insistence, like caged canaries at the bird market. Mrs Vernon looked like a parrot chained to its perch, with grey feathers and red eyes. Next to her was Mrs Elsa. I don't know if she was still wearing her night gown, because she had got hold of a coat from somewhere. It was too big for her, even with the buttons done up and the sleeves rolled back. She turned around again and again, peering up at the Peak behind. I knew what she was doing. She was thinking of Mari, unable to prevent herself from trying to catch a glimpse of our apartment windows, tiny as they were from here. Over the last few days this gesture must have become a nervous tic, because the captain, who was standing next to her, put his hand on her shoulder to stop her.

Then she looked up and saw me. I was standing with Lam and Wang and Wei on a small rise towards the south side of the parade ground. Even though it was overrun by this time, and she was maybe twenty rows into the crowd, I could make her out clearly. I saw the pain in her face. I wanted to make some kind of gesture to show that Mari was all right, tucked safely away on my back, but there were Japanese soldiers moving through the crowd with clipboards and pens, taking details, then gathering together in little groups out front with their heads together. They wore loose-fitting military jackets, and long boots to the knee. They had canvas peaked hats that sat on top of their heads like one of Mrs Elsa's china pepper pots. They seemed happy enough for us to stand at the edges of the ground and stare at our captured masters. But when a man close to us stepped out of our line dragging a heavy trunk over to his master, who had positioned himself on the outer edges of the group, one of the soldiers appeared instantly and started hitting the English man over the head with the back of a bayonet, until he fell over. I saw Mrs Elsa glance over again, and she must have caught sight of Mari's goose-feather hair sticking up over my shoulder, for the expression on her face contracted, then loosened.

'How are we going to get their things to them? And Mari?'
I said to Wei.

He put a finger to his lips and pushed his way out of the
throng of silent spectators around us. He went straight up to
the Japanese soldier at the head of the group of prisoners, and
started speaking to him confidently, as if he had arranged to
meet him by appointment. Wei had taken a bath that morning
in the apartment, and a blue-black line of sunlight reflected
off his hair as he spoke to the soldier. He was wearing one of
the captain's shirts open at the collar, and a pair of Wang's
chauffeuring trousers. His pockets were bulging with the
money we'd found rolled up in the top drawer of Mrs Elsa's
dressing table.

There was a woman at my elbow, with wild grey hair that
was neither plaited nor in a bun.

'You're lucky your man is rich,' she said.

I thought at first she was talking about the captain, then I
realised she was talking about Wei, about the ease with which
the soldier accepted the money from him, like a waiter
accepting a night's wages by way of a tip from a generous
customer. He gestured for Wei to come over to where I was
standing with Wang and Lam, each of us with one of the
packed suitcases at our feet.

Mr Tommy saw Wang, and walked over to us, slowly, so that
he wouldn't attract too much attention from anyone apart from
the soldier who'd given permission for this exchange to take
place. He put a hand to Mari's cheek.

'Sir,' said Wang. 'I'm sorry.'

The captain shook his head.

'You couldn't have stopped them.'

'Where are they taking you, Sir?' Wang asked. His voice was
full of a concern which I suspected was as much for himself as
for anyone else.

'No one knows,' said the captain. He swallowed once or twice in quick succession, as if he needed a drink of water. 'They've had us under lock and key in a bloody slum for the past week.'

'Sir,' I said, showing him the bags at our feet. 'We went back to the apartment. We have clothes for you.'

Mari's breath on the back of my neck was hotter than the morning air around us.

'God bless you,' Mr Tommy said. 'I'll take the bags and one of you follow a few paces behind with Mari. We don't want to antagonise the bastards.'

He picked up all three of the bags.

I had been trying to imagine how this moment would feel, when I would have to say goodbye to Mari, but I couldn't feel anything. The air was already filled with the scent of her leaving: her special baby shampoo, her formula milk, and soap flakes – the comforting mixed-up smells that always stuck to the skin under my fingernails after a day spent taking care of her.

Wei seemed to know all this as if I had been sitting there with him at his stall dictating it to him for a cent. Before I knew it, his swollen, callused fingers had undone the strap and taken her off my back and he was gone, through the crowd after the captain like a pickpocket, light on his feet.

I held my breath as he made his way with the captain over to Mrs Elsa, but she had moved, shifted by the surge of the crowd all around her. I looked back at Wei, but he had disappeared from sight too, lost among lowered heads and trails of cigarette smoke. Then I caught sight of Mrs Elsa again, picked out from the crowd by a weak ray of winter sun that reminded me of the dusty bands of light in the shuttered bars Ryan used to favour. She stood with her arms held out, her eyes dry, waiting. As Wei came back into view, slipping Mari into her arms, I felt as if my own skin was being unpeeled from my flesh, strip by strip. I thought of the dead woman on the pavement outside the bombed arcade, her hand in her dead son's.

Mari was awake, her hands grabbing at Mrs Elsa's hair, and they were smiling at each other. I could only see them from the side now, half of Mrs Elsa's smile, and half of Mari's: two halves of the same smile.

The soldier Wei had paid off seemed to have lost the goodwill we had paid him for.

'Hurry up,' he called over. Within seconds Wei was back at my side. He didn't even seem short of breath.

My back was cold.

Lam and Wang were arguing with Wei, saying that he should have kept some of the money for us, that we needed it too, but all my attention was taken up by Mari. She looked different from a distance. I stared at her, trying to impress upon my memory the dense blue of her eyes, the red patch of eczema on her chin that always bothers her unless I put cream on it, her fingers that open and close constantly, trying to hold all of the life that surrounds her in her hungry, uncertain grasp.

The soldiers had given up on the task of taking names and papers. A command went out for everyone to dispose of their identification, and to start marching. As the prisoners shuffled off the ground they left behind them a mosaic of navy-blue squares speckled across the lush grass.

'British passports,' said Wei.

We followed, and the soldiers did nothing to stop us. It was as if they wanted us to be in no doubt about who our new masters would be. The pavements outside the parade ground were already full of people like us, newly unemployed and not quite sure what to do with themselves except watch. We managed to find our way through the crowd to a space along

Connaught Road where the crush had eased off. We positioned ourselves on the pavement and watched like everyone else. The British were walking ten across with their heads down. One man looked up and a Japanese soldier punched him straight in the face and he looked down again. Blood dripped from his nose onto the pavement. A dog ran over from the crowd and sniffed the blood and the soldier shot it without hesitation. The dog's corpse fell limply to the ground.

There were two launches on the quay. The engines were running and smoke throttled out in a cloud over the *sampans* tied onto them at the back with towing ropes. The prisoners were herded up the gangplanks like goats, so many of them that I couldn't even see the captain and Mrs Elsa and Mari any more.

We didn't wait to watch the boats leave. Instead, we went back to see what was left of our *kongsi fong*. As we walked I put a hand in my pocket where I'd kept one of Mari's bonnets, the size of a bird's nest, and a letter to you, Third Sister, that I'd taken to the post office that morning, only to be told it was closed until further notice.

III

Tommy:
Captain Thomas Owen Jones Logbook

STANLEY INTERNMENT CAMP
HONG KONG ISLAND
1942

5th January

Embark Victoria 11.00 am. Set sail 11.30. Hold course due south through Lamma Channel. Arrive Stanley 2.00 pm.

6th January

22° 13' 00" N, 114° 12' 00" E

Stanley Peninsula: one fishing village of unknown population, one purpose-built prison for Hong Kong criminals, one preparatory school known as St Stephen's College, and Stanley Fort. Enemy aliens – British, Dutch and American – to be interned in the college and some of the prison's outlying buildings. Prison itself to be retained for detention of Chinese miscreants from the city. New barbed wire fences already in place around the denoted areas.

Thirteen buildings to house over three thousand captured civilians. Assigned with Elsa to former Indian warders' quarters overlooking Tytam Bay: ten people to a room of 14 x 10 feet, no bedding except our two wool blankets, which must be used as mattresses. Men and women to sleep separately. Shower, toilet and kitchen to be shared between at least six. Mosquitoes.

Supper: rice stew and cabbage.

7th January

Turn to at 6.00 am. First job is to clear up, starting in the science labs, wrecked during fighting. (Soldiers and Red Cross nurses maimed, raped, killed by Japs, then burned. Ash heap with bones sticking out of it still smoking in the exercise yard: our men or theirs, we don't know.) Broken glass, brown and blue, all over the grass outside. Inside: dried blood on walls and floors, mud and plaster, exploded sandbags, glass, military buttons. Toilets overflowing.

Bodies – a few British, twenty-odd Canadians. Canadians still chubby with puppy fat, freckled to hell by the sun. We go through their pockets before we bury them. One of them has a letter folded up without an envelope. *From your loving Mother.* Bury it with him in the cemetery on the hill. Beyond the barbed wire a sea so bright it burns the blue out of the sky. We don't know if they would do things differently in Canada, so we do things our way. *Ashes to ashes. Dust to dust.*

10th January

Five days in we can still smell death, although the bodies have been buried. We forage through each building in turn, collecting any utensils we can find: knives, forks, tin cups, maybe enough for three hundred people. Oscar Campbell says it's a start. When I ask him how he thinks it will finish he says that such questions are best avoided. Women and children and all that. I see him keeping a nervous eye on them, wondering if they are going to be more of a hindrance than a help. Elsa sits in the yard below our quarters holding Mari, staring into space. When I ask her what's wrong, she says, 'I should have left her with Lin. She would have been better off with Lin.'

Campbell and I agree at least that there has to be some sort of order here. Organisation from the top down, a plan of action. He says we need to set up a committee, and asks me if I'd like to be on it. His superior attitude gets under my skin. I say yes. Mimi says if anyone should be in charge around here, it's me.

24th January

Mari needs clean water to drink. I turn to at 5.00 am to start boiling it up so it will cool by the time she wakes. I watch as she sits on Elsa's lap, sipping it off a spoon, crying for milk. There isn't any. Elsa gives her more water. I walk around the camp with a few of my good clothes that Lin packed for me. I find a Dutch woman who managed to bring five tins of powdered milk with her for her toddler. She lets me have two of them in exchange for a pair of golfing trousers and a Norfolk jacket.

First meeting of the Temporary Committee at 10.00 am. Officers elected by a show of hands, and blackboard and chalk used to note names and votes. A full and proper election to be put on once we are settled. Top of the list will be a housing committee, canteen committee and medical committee, plus entertainment (Campbell is of the opinion that distractions are necessary). We attach names to groups, start to establish boundaries.

The Japs do likewise. They distribute a copy of regulations. We are informed that their treatment of us will be dependent on the treatment of Nipponese prisoners-of-war at the hands of the American, British and Dutch governments. We are to form self-cooperative unions in our quarters, each with its own department head. We are ordered not to leave the camp, look down over the prison grounds below, use the football ground, or pick flowers. If any internist should break these regulations, they will be punished according to military law.

I ask Elsa if she wants to head up the entertainment committee, maybe get a theatre troupe going, raise people's spirits, but she shakes her head.

'Oscar Campbell said I could help set up a sanatorium,' she says.

'Are you sure that's a good idea? What about the risk of infection for Mari?'

'Nobody's infected with anything, are they?'

'Not yet.'

'It's what I want to do.'

'Fine, then. Go ahead and do it.'

I'll bet these niggles are going on all over the camp – couples arguing over inconsequential matters so we don't have to face up to everything else. The future is a blank, and no number of committees is going to change that.

17th February

I walk around the inside perimeter of the fence every day, getting my bearings. Mimi likes to come with me most days. Safety in numbers, she says. The camp takes up the heel of the peninsula, separated from the rest of Hong Kong Island by the village. The pump house and fort lie on the other side, looking over the South China Sea. Our quarters are grouped around the prison proper, but separated from it by the wire. The only buildings that overlook the prison directly are the Japanese headquarters, which have been set up in the former superintendent's house. I manage to get a surreptitious glimpse of the yard below one day, when no one's looking, and see a few Chinese cons walking aimlessly around the exercise yard.

I'm starting to understand the lie of the land. Inside the wire are five bungalows with roofs shaped like coolie hats, designated A to E, occupied by high-up civil servants, doctors and the like who seem to have brought their hierarchy with them. Oscar Campbell is among their number; I can tell he feels slightly ashamed of this self-imposed privilege. Grouped around the Jap headquarters are several large stucco-and-tile accommodation blocks, which have been split into American, British and Dutch billets. Each nationality organises its own kitchens. The land is surrounded by Tytam Bay to the east, Tweed Bay to the south, and Stanley Bay to the west.

On the western side of the peninsula, behind the old school buildings, are the school tennis courts, already overgrown. There must be something in my blood that makes my fingers tingle when I see the long grass on the courts, and the row of young lemon trees around one of its edges. The farmer in me. It's what my father does. It's what everyone does where I come from, once they get too old for their captain's uniform. And it's what I'll do too, when I get out of this bastard place.

The grass doesn't have the drenched smell of the grass at home, but it's good to stand in the feeble winter sun and feel it beneath my feet. I'm at the northern limit of the camp, so close to the village I can see the police station. Between the wire and Tytam Bay there are large warehouses – or godowns, as they call them over here – set close to the water at regular intervals. This is where the Japs keep their own supplies, impossible to break in without getting shot at. They are full to the brim with tins of spam, oatmeal, sugar tablets, meat broth. You can practically read the bloody labels through the windows from here.

Seems someone must have been feeling generous today, though, as lunch is a cause for excitement: tinned tomatoes. We give the lion's share to the children: one whole tomato each. They beam as they suck on the sour juice, crunching the seeds. My stomach is rumbling, bubbling emptily.

'Stop!' I say to one boy, holding a hand up.

His mother looks annoyed.

'Spit the seeds out.' I hold out my tin can, and the boy gobs them into it along with a mouthful of saliva. I get the other youngsters to do the same. In the end I have maybe thirty or forty unspoiled seeds. I go to Campbell and hold out the can for his inspection.

'We need to start a vegetable garden,' I say.

19th February

The Nips have to be handled carefully, says Campbell. We can't just go making demands and expecting them to be satisfied without quibbling. We have to take things slowly.

In the meantime my precious seeds will grow mould if I don't get them in the ground soon. I smuggle bricks and earth up to the roof of our quarters, handful by handful. I build a raised bed, fill it with soil. I make shallow indentations in the earth with my thumb at regular intervals, press a seed into each one, and cover it over. I water them twice a day. I wait. I don't hold out much hope. The soil here is poor, rocky, more or less infertile; you can tell just from looking at the bare outcrops of eroded rocks scattered over the edges of the camp. Not much grows here, apart from a few trees. And the flowers. There are bulb orchids in bloom already, pushing out purple buds, hibiscus too, and it looks as if there will be camellias and rhododendrons on the way soon, if all those glossy-leaved bushes fulfil their promise. If we were allowed to pick flowers someone would have had a go at making soup from them by now. It would be worth a try. Anything's worth a try.

Lizzie Vernon is head of the canteen committee. She keeps a record of each meal we're provided with, by portion and food group. The rice comes in sacks, uncooked. Once we've been through it and picked out the live weevils, cigarettes butts and other rubbish, it weighs about a quarter less than it did when it arrived on the ration truck. Yesterday there was a dead rat in there. I didn't tell Elsa. Last week there was meat of a kind we've never eaten before – water buffalo, for God's sake – all gristle and bone and not much flesh. Fish is delivered frozen, but is decayed all the same by the time we unload it.

It's an hour and twenty-five minutes since morning congee. Three hours and thirty-five minutes to go until lunch. The last sixty minutes are the worst. By then my hunger will have subsided to a grinding ache that threatens to scrape out my insides. I know that much already.

From up here I can see the children doing their lessons in the open air, sitting in cross-legged rows. An education committee has been set up, all plain-faced, do-gooding women of the type I could do without, but at least the children are being kept occupied. Some of them scratch their heads from time to time. Lice. We'll have to shave their hair right back. Get hold of disinfectant from somewhere. Elsa says there's nothing at the hospital yet, apart from a bit of quinine, but Mimi's heard on the grapevine that the Red Cross will get a few parcels through before long.

1st March

Mari's birthday. St David's Day. The pine trees are starting to shed their needles. I make a rough composting box from bamboo canes and odd bits of board and start to heap all the greenery together to make leaf mould. It will take a while to rot down into half-decent mulch, but it will improve the soil, if nothing else. Campbell says that talking to people about planting seeds that will take months to come to anything is just going to depress them when we are all going round camp in-between meals chewing grass because we are so hungry. 'Not everyone's chewing grass,' I say to him. There's a black market on the go, and people who came in here with a stash of money are able to buy cigarettes and even boiled sweets. Lord knows where they come from. All I know is that we don't have the cash and Mari's milk has run out again. Elsa and Lizzie Vernon have tried crushing soya beans to make a substitute, but their experiments haven't been too successful so far. Elsa says she just needs a bit of practice, but Mari is pale and she cries. She should be crawling around the place by now, but she seems to sense that she needs to conserve her energy, and she spends most of the day sitting still on a blanket close to wherever Elsa is working. 'Don't worry,' the other women shout over to Elsa if she gets called away on an errand. 'We'll keep an eye on her.' But the truth is that nobody needs to keep an eye on Mari because she's still sitting in exactly the same place when Elsa gets back.

Mari was born a year ago today. Elsa makes a spice cake out of ground rice flour. It tastes worse than bad, but we eat it because we are hungry and it is an extra ration, allowed by the canteen committee in honour of Mari's birthday.

20th April

The camp is being run by a couple of jokers – on the Jap side of things, I mean. Kobayashi was the barber at the Hong Kong Hotel before the war. He was there for donkey's years, according to Campbell, even gave Campbell a wet shave once. The other one, Fujimoto, worked as a tailor's assistant in Wan Chai for five years. That's how far ahead of us they were. Makes me sick to the gullet to think about it.

Fujimoto has ditched his general's uniform for linen suits, striped in pale colours and double-breasted, too big for him all over. He oils his hair back from his face, which is thin and long as a weasel's, with the same thin-lipped grin. Kob is more difficult to get the measure of. There's something boyish about him. He holds his sunhat across his stomach as if it were a football, and he wears short trousers and socks rolled down to the knee. They look quite ridiculous together, trotting around the camp. Mimi and I sometimes bump into them when we are doing our rounds, and we ignore each other.

But today they are making a beeline for me. They've taken to keeping dogs; long lean wolfhounds with heads too big for their bodies. They let them run ahead, off the lead and laugh when they see groups of children scrambling out of the way, frightened. Those two are a pair of sadistic bastards, even under their sheep's clothing.

I am chopping logs out in the exercise yard. We get given a catty – about a pound and a half – of firewood a day, and although the weather's getting pretty warm, we still need to keep the fires going to cook food and boil water.

'Bridge,' Fuji says to me. Kob refuses to speak English. Seems he decided to dump his enemies' language as soon as he was no longer required to hand out a short back and sides with a smile, and accept paltry tips from rich white men.

I wonder what the hell they're talking about. I'm buggered if I'm going to call him Sir, so I just stand there with the head of the axe resting at my feet, looking down. If you don't do that you get a clip to the back of the head.

One of the dogs sniffs at the tip of the axe and whines. Fuji strokes its glossy fur.

'We want to play bridge, and we want you and your wife and Dr Campbell to join us,' he says.

I cough.

'That would make a five and not a four,' I say, wondering if I can bluff my way through this one. I never did bridge or whist in Hong Kong – I left all that to Elsa, although she complained that bridge was for fat old women and that she was only going along with it to please me. She used to make me laugh when she said that kind of thing.

Fuji tells me to bring Elsa and Campbell with me to their headquarters at 7.00 pm. I go and find Campbell, expecting him to say that this is it, our chance to make a stand, show the bastards who's boss.

'But they are the ones who are in charge,' he says to me.

'Not if we take to our arms and bloody well fight,' I say. 'There are three thousand of us.'

113

He shakes his head. He looks far too relaxed, as if he's in a holiday camp, for God's sake.

'What arms? It's over, Tom,' he says, friendly enough.

'So what are we here for?' I counter. I'm determined to have a fight with someone. If not with him, then one of the generals.

'We're here because they've got no idea what to do with us. Civilians. The worst kind of prisoner.'

'So we just do nothing?'

Elsa comes out of the kitchens. The door doubles back on its hinges and bangs against the wall. She comes straight at me, puts a hand on my arm. I feel a mixture of desire and rage as I pull away from her.

'Tommy.' She sounds embarrassed.

'Look, Tom,' Campbell says in that annoyingly easy tone of his. 'All we can count on until we hear otherwise is ourselves.'

If Mimi had been with me she'd have given them a bollocking. She wouldn't have put up with this either.

The superintendent's house has a plain but impressively large porchway, and a verandah running right around the building on the first floor, with the roof jutting out above. As we walk up the drive, someone inside switches the lights on. For a moment, it's like going to any party, anywhere, on a bad night when everything's already gone wrong; trying to muster up the energy to socialise, to laugh at jokes that aren't funny, and smile at people you don't like.

The house has either been left untouched by the fighting, or they've done a better job than us at clearing up. We are taken into a large room with a view over Tweed Bay, and a parquet floor. There is a table set out for us in the middle of the room, with five rattan chairs around it. A lamp hangs low over the table, throwing out an oblong of light. I haven't seen an electric bulb for a while. It makes me blink.

Fuji gestures at me to sit with him and Kob.

'General Kobayashi will observe us this evening,' he says. 'You can teach him by playing in a pair with me.'

'How much do you know of the game already?' I ask, hoping that it's less than I do. If so, I'll be free to make things up as I go along, and send them back to Tokyo with some cock-and-bull version, and no one need know any different.

'Some,' he says, running a hand through his hair.

I can see that Elsa is scared stiff. She shuffles the cards face down, staring down at their red-and-white chevrons, and deals two hands, one for Fuji and me, the other for her and Campbell. Kob sits just behind me, looking over my shoulder.

Elsa considers her hand, points something out to Campbell silently, but he shows little interest. This isn't his kind of thing at all. He seems quieter than usual, quite thoughtful. His big ears stick out at the sides of his face like door handles and his ginger hair is growing down over his ears. We are all starting to look uncared for, even Elsa. Her hair is straggled and dirty.

She spreads out a vertical column of cards on the table.

'Diamonds,' she says.

Fuji inclines his head towards me, as if this is a serious business and he trusts me to give him the information he needs. I whisper some bullshit about bids and contracts and tell him we should pass. He follows my instructions to the letter. We win. I suspect Elsa is also adapting her game to the current circumstances, to make sure we arrive at the required result.

'Milk,' she says, spreading out her final hand. Her fingers are trembling. 'I need powdered milk for my little girl.'

I see Campbell looking at her, and wonder what he'll say afterwards.

Fuji grins, showing his perfect teeth and the tip of his thick, pink tongue. He turns back towards the sideboard to get a pack of cigarettes.

'Of course,' he says, flipping back the top of his lighter. 'May I offer you a drink?' A servant comes out of the shadows in the corner of the room and serves us whisky on the rocks. His soft-soled shoes make a slapping sound on the floor as he moves round the table. There's a wireless on the sideboard behind him, with pillar-like strips at each side, the white circle of its tuner like a compass in the middle, and two black dials below. It would be so easy to lean over, flick the switch.

The whisky hits the back of my tongue like a fireball.

I clear my throat.

'I was wondering what you plan to do with the old tennis courts,' I ask.

Fuji and Kob look at each other. Fuji has drunk his whisky too quickly and has reverted to the same position he's been sitting in most of the night, his cards in one hand and the other folded into his arm. He looks like an old woman knitting.

'Nothing,' Kob says, his eyes thinner than his lips. Seems he remembers his English when he really needs to.

'I was wondering if we could turn it into a garden. Grow vegetables and the like.'

Campbell is looking at me. I can tell how nervous he is, that he regrets not having the guts to come out with this himself.

No one says anything. The room seems too bright: the electric lights, the new wireless on the sideboard.

Finally Fuji says, 'Yes. Do what you can with it.'

They offer us another whisky and we all accept. Even Campbell is more animated than I've ever seen him as we walk back to our quarters.

'Well done, my man,' he keeps saying. 'Great stuff.'

Elsa laughs intermittently, the way she used to at parties. As I walk ahead of her and Campbell I feel like the tallest person in the camp and I start to sing 'Bread of Heaven'. Elsa groans and apologises to Campbell, her voice affectionate – 'He likes a song when he's drunk.' One of the guards lets a shot out of a gun across the fence that they are watching night and day to stop Chinese black marketeers selling us fags and sugar. I stop singing.

28th June

I turn to at six most mornings. The sun rises furiously in the sky, grabbing the day by its throat. The camp is silent as I walk through the quarters over to the tennis courts. I work without thinking, turning clods of earth with a two-pronged fork which has to do the job for now, and by the time the whistle is blown for congee I realise that two hours have passed.

Campbell says I'm to have top-up rations, as will anyone else who commits to working at least five hours a day with me. The promise of extra food is enough. Soon there's a group of men with me in the mornings, walking over the rise from the Indian quarters.

We plant anything we can get our hands on. If our rations include fresh tomatoes, or melons – which are a rarity – the flesh is often puckered and spoiled, bleeding juice, but the women who work in the kitchens cut out the seeds and pass them on to us. People with friends in Hong Kong get them to send bulbs in their relief parcels. Although they are confiscated on arrival more often than not, the occasional packet gets through.

Before long there are rows of green seedlings emerging out of the earth, and runner beans climbing up bamboo poles. Once I've made a start, there's no stopping me. We have a go at corn, eggplant and beet spinach. The tomatoes are doing well. My rooftop plants have started to take, and I transfer them to the larger plot. It's too early to put root vegetables in, but I'll put carrot tops straight into the earth when the time comes, and I may even give *paak tsoi* and peanuts a try.

'We could end up being completely self-sufficient at this rate. No more kowtowing to the Japs,' I say to Elsa.

She's sitting next to me above the Indian warders' quarters, cutting down a pair of my trousers to make them into shorts. Three sewing machines survived the fighting, and the women pass them round the camp as and when they need them. Needle and thread are coming through from the Red Cross, although not as much as they would like. The kids are constantly growing out of their clothes, despite the poor rations, and anyway a lot of the mothers seem to enjoy sewing for the sake of it, just to pass the time. They'd make clothes out of anything. A young woman walked past me yesterday wearing a sun top put together from flour sacks, embroidered with pink flowers around the edges where the sacking met the pale white mound of her breasts. She was carrying a bag of rice from the ration distribution garage over to the kitchens, leaning forward to take the weight of it on her back. One of the corners of the bag had split and the rice poured out like water from a leaking tap. A group of children ran after her and fell upon it avidly, stuffing it into their mouths, and pushing each other away. They swallowed it so fast it made some of them choke, so that in the end they had to use their fists to tap each other on the back, and watch half-chewed, off-white kernels spray their way through the air and land in the dirt at their feet. The girl carried on walking, taking no notice, her firm buttocks sticking out of her tight shorts like ripe greengages.

'Come for a walk with me, *cariad*,' I say to Elsa, putting a hand over hers, feeling the needle catch against my skin.

'I can't,' she says.

'Why not?'

'What about Mari? I can't just leave her.'

'She's fast asleep, isn't she?'

'Yes, I know, but she's got this cough.'

'What cough?' I sit up.

'It's all right,' Elsa says. 'The duty doctor said it was a slight chest infection, and Oscar Campbell's signed a chitty for her to be given a multivitamin tablet every day. But she gets this tickle in her throat, and she's been waking up at night, needing water.'

The sun is setting over Tweed Bay, and the heat is starting to drain out of the day. In the distance two figures wearing pointed hats are carrying nets slung over their shoulders towards one of the boats in the shallows. They bend over as they work. The nets look like sails folded up on themselves. One of the men has his trousers rolled up. The other one is wearing wellingtons. The one in wellingtons starts to disentangle a bundle of rope in the boat. They both get in, gingerly, as if they are getting on a bit, although it is hard to see from here with the sun behind them. One of them sits in the stern of the boat, still unsnarling the rope that runs from one hand to the other in knots, while the other one stands up and starts to push the boat out to deeper water with an oar.

'You should have told me,' I say. 'Straightaway, so I could have done something.'

'You're always so busy with that garden,' says Elsa.

'What do you mean, *that* garden, as if it's got nothing to do with you?'

She glances at me, then back at her needlework. The stitches she makes are small and even. She always holds the material close to her eyes to push the needle through it. In Hong Kong I kept telling her she should get around to wearing glasses, but she never did anything about it. She said she quite liked seeing life that way, blurred at the edges. It's true there were certain things she seemed never to want to examine too closely, even her own image in the mirror, so it couldn't have been pure vanity, or laziness.

'It's a hell of a risk, that's all,' she says. Her intonation is so similar to Campbell's when she says it that I know exactly which horse's mouth to blame. That is so like him, with his pursed-lipped, *slowly slowly* response to everything.

Fair enough, then. I won't tell her what else is hidden in the garden. I was going to confide in her and no one else, but the haughty shadows the twilight draws across her face make me feel as if I'm looking at her from a distance, under a spotlight, observing everything about her I don't like: her near-sighted desire just to see what she wants to see, her naïve, blind trust in the people who run the show, like Campbell, and her newfound enthusiasm for playing at Florence Nightingale on her day shifts at the sanatorium.

So I keep it to myself, my secret. Those seeds in the garden have to bear fruit, not just to stop us all from starving, but because I've got another plan on the go, one that I haven't shared with Campbell and his pals.

I've been sending messages out of camp, glued into the insides of the van driver's cigarette packets. Packages come back in on the ration trucks, in clean bed sheets wrapped up tight to conceal the leads and plugs inside. I take them and hide them in the garden, deep in the earth under my tidy rows of onions and dwarf beans. I'm the only one who knows where all the components are buried. I crouch down on the damp earth. While Campbell and Elsa and all the rest of them are feasting on pea soup, I'll be building my own wireless, finding the right frequency to get us out of here.

But I have to wait, that's the problem. Work and wait. And no one else seems to have the patience to wait with me, apart from Mimi. I know I can trust her, at least. They all think we'll be out in a few weeks. And then, as one month gives way to the next, and we acquire layers of sunburn that makes us look older and tougher, they start saying that it'll be the end of the year.

'We'll be out by Christmas,' I hear people saying to Campbell in the queue for food at the canteen. 'You'll make sure of that, won't you, Sir?'

'I will most certainly do my best,' he says in that slick way he has of saying something that is clearly not the truth but sounds closer to it than anyone else will ever get. That's why people trust him, let him lead.

'You do have faith in me, don't you?' I say to Elsa, tightening my grip on her hand, the needle digging deeper into my skin.

'Of course.' She pulls away to gather up her sewing things and gets to her feet. 'I'm just going to look in on Mari.'

There's a drop of blood on the palm of my hand where the needle pricked it, but it wipes away easily enough. I meant to sit and wait for her to come back, but I'm tired and aching all over. I get to my feet too, make my way to the quarters and fall onto my blanket without even splashing my face. It's a toss-up between hunger and fatigue most nights. If I stay up too long after we've had our evening meal I can't sleep. I end up chewing the bloody blankets to fill my mouth with saliva, in the hope it will make me feel something in my stomach. But if I go to bed straight after supper, there's no time to see or talk to anyone, even Elsa, especially Elsa, no human interaction to distinguish one day's hard labour from the next. Mari is sprouting before my eyes like a potato plant, and yet I'm so tired I hardly get to take any notice.

15th August

Now we are all waiting.

I sit under the shelter of the pine trees in the cemetery with Mimi, her hand resting on my knee. It's quiet up here, with nobody much around. I get my list out and take another look at it. I consult it so frequently that it feels odd if it isn't there, folded up in my right-hand trouser pocket, the corners starting to rub and wear away. Soon enough I'll have to copy it out again. But I even enjoy that – borrowing pen and paper from Campbell and sitting down to go through my graph one more time, using a light-coloured pencil to indicate sowing times and a dark-coloured pen to show when the crops should be ready.

It's almost time. Parsnips as misshapen as withered old men on park benches show me the firmest, whitest flesh when I break them open with my knife. Lemons like waxed suns start falling from the trees of their own accord, and I have to tick them off my list sooner than expected and go round camp begging for a basket to gather them in. The cucumbers are longer and thinner than they should be, with lumpy skins, but each slice streams with fresh juice.

Next to floppy ears of Ceylon spinach on the vine are rows of brassica and chard. I can already taste the tough green stems. I rub celery leaves together between my fingers and hold them to my nose. Gooseberries have sprung up with the help of makeshift canes; a few loose clusters have started falling to the ground with a soft thwock, splitting open to reveal their translucent husks. The golden skins of onions the size of my fist are on the verge of breaking and peeling away from the layers inside.

It is Sunday night and I walk around the garden, checking on my produce. Soon it will be brought into the kitchens to be chopped, pickled, preserved, bottled, jellied, or just eaten. I kneel down and breathe in the smell of roots growing and holding onto the soil, not letting go until their work is done. I feel around among the tubers with my fingers, discreetly, so no one will notice. It's still there, my underground network of electrical components. One or two may have been spoiled in the sudden rainstorm that blew southwards over the peninsula last week, but I'm happy to bet it's mostly good to be harvested along with the rest. This is the perfect time: Kob and Fuji have become fattened and lazy. They even pant as they try to keep up with their pet dogs.

I see Elsa's tall shadow coming towards me. I straighten up before she notices the knobbled earth underneath our feet where, under the criss-cross of cabbage stalks, metal rods protrude here and there like the ribs of an underfed child.

She offers me a cigarette.

'Where d'you get them?' I say, as we saunter up to the top of the cemetery.

'One of the doctors gave me a couple of packs.'

There's been a dysentery outbreak in the main school building. Lizzie Vernon offered to sit with Mari so Elsa could work round the clock at the sanatorium, sitting by people's beds, mopping their hands and faces at regular intervals, fetching Campbell if they seemed to be getting worse. During the day the women who work in the laundry room have been flat out washing sheets and hanging them across the yards to dry, kids skipping in and out of them, making ghost noises and jumping out at each other from behind the damp linen.

I take a fag off Elsa as we sit down. We smoke with our backs against the trunk of a casuarina tree, listening to the breeze ruffling its leaves. Elsa is much skinnier than she used to be. Even her fingers are as thin as string. Her hands look like my mother's: dry and wrinkled and bleached by soap flakes. They are hands that work hard. But lying back like this holding her cigarette, she reminds me of how she was before I married her. She had a smooth exterior, but she was unsophisticated, just another one of the village girls who were so easily impressed by my naval uniform and gifts from exotic places. We got married pretty quick – a shotgun wedding, Mam called it. When I asked Elsa if she would marry me she said yes straightaway, then cried, as if she'd been waiting for me to pop the question for all of the three months we had been fully acquainted. She cried on our wedding day, too.

I stub my cigarette out on the grass and roll over onto my front.

'God, my shoulders are aching.'

'Here, let me rub them for you,' she says, balancing her cigarette on a rock and rolling up her sleeves. She bends over me and lifts the back of my shirt. She presses her fingers into the muscles at the base of my back, then pummels her way up either side of my spine to my shoulders. The knots in my back loosen abruptly, making me groan. Her hands travel back down my back, lightly this time. She skims her fingertips all the way down my back, feeling her way round to my crotch. She smells of something bitter, like thiamine. Something from the medicine cabinet at that bloody hospital.

Instead of rolling over and pulling her on top of me, I shift and turn away. I wait for her to ask me what's wrong, but she doesn't. She picks up her cigarette and takes another drag on it, looking over the shallow bay.

20th August

Bridge is the last thing on anyone's mind, apart from Fuji and Kob. Elsa and Campbell and I are called over to headquarters at weekly intervals for a round of cards and whisky. When other people get to hear of it as a regular thing there's a bit of leg-pulling, until they get jealous.

'In with the Japs, are we?'

'Playing cards with the Nips, eh?'

'And what do you get in return, that's what I'd like to know?'

We are getting quite a bit in return, by now. As well as the garden, there is a regular supply of medicine coming in – far too little to keep everyone healthy, but it's something, as

Campbell says. It also keeps the Nips in a good mood, which is no bad thing. Parade is a long and miserable process when they are ill-tempered. People are pulled out of line, knocked about, and pushed back again. Elsa tries to hold Mari so that she can't see, but she swivels her little head and watches as people are batted down to the ground with the edge of a bayonet. It's usually men, but sometimes women. When they found out that a couple of girls were offering their services around the camp in return for a tin of bully beef, they hauled them out to the front, made them strip and slapped them about. I was standing behind Campbell. I heard him clearing his throat and saw a vein swelling in the back of his neck. I kept quiet too. Perhaps I'm coming round to his way of thinking. The greater good, that's his argument. And he and I will be no use to the three thousand people here if we get shot for the sake of a couple of prostitutes. So we watch like everyone else as their clothes are ripped off them and they are smacked across the face. Poor kids. They're only kids after all. Scrawny too, now. The Japs tell them that will be the last time they indulge in any monkey business. The truth is they'll be at it again before you can say how's your father. And their customers aren't just Brits who are missing their wives. They've had a few Japs, I'd say, and although they cry themselves to pieces when they're being embarrassed and beaten about in front of everyone, chances are they're crocodile tears that will dry up quickly enough when their Jap boyfriends offer them a bit of consolation in the shelter of one of the godowns after dark tonight.

'Poor girls,' Elsa says, as we walk over to the superintendent's house for our bridge session.

Campbell says nothing. He's such a stuffed bloody shirt.

'I'm getting sick of this,' I say.

'What?' Elsa sounds tetchy.

'Turning up here every week like lapdogs and getting hardly anything in return.'

'We don't have much choice,' Campbell says.

The session doesn't go well. I am getting better at this stupid card game, but Elsa seems to be getting worse. She's not used to being in company any more. She watches everyone else as they play instead of studying her own cards, biting her nails and chewing the skin at the edges of her fingers. Fuji and Kob don't seem to notice; they are distracted tonight too. They had whisky served the moment we came in, but didn't offer us any. Now they are scratching their heads over their cards, blinking and yawning. Kob has put the radio on, I don't know to which station. A woman's alto voice croons in the background.

'Elsa, dear.'

There's something about Campbell's tone that reminds me of the variety show put on by the entertainment committee in the canteen the night before. It's a notch louder than it should be. I was never one for amateur dramatics, but it was good to see the kids enjoying themselves at least, dressed up in wigs made of unravelled rope and costume jewellery fashioned from corned-beef tins.

She glances at him, lets her hand drop into her lap. She moves closer to observe the cards with him. He turns to her and asks, 'Shall we pass this time, do you think?'

It is as she nods her agreement that the penny drops.

They are sleeping together.

I stare down at my cards and watch as the black clubs merge into spades. I know that if they were alone he would put his hand over her chewed fingers and tell her that he loves her. I'm about to stand up and start roaring the place down – I don't give a shit what Fuji and Kob think, they can bloody well shoot me for all I care – when the door is opened, and two men walk straight at us. There is a pop and a flash in my face and I think I must be about to die, my bloody heart is jumping about so much, and then I smell the acidic vapour of magnesium burning off, and see the round silver circle of a camera bulb, flat as a frying pan.

Fuji gets up and turns the radio off. There is a small boom inside the box, and an amplified click before it goes quiet.

'We have visitors,' he says, showing his teeth, 'This is Mr Tan of the *Hong Kong News*. He's come to write an article about Stanley.'

I see Campbell weighing up the situation. I see Elsa looking at him too, a look that burns a hardwired filament right through my heart, scorching me from the inside out.

'Sirs, Madam,' says a Chinese man carrying a fedora and notebook, coming forward and shaking hands with us in turn.

We sit around. The cards stare up at us from the table.

'So life is pretty good in here, you would say?'

The journalist turns to Campbell first.

Campbell's orange hair has been burned to blond by the sun. His forearms are covered in sunspots.

'Reasonable.' He looks straight at the journalist to let him know how far off the mark this one word is, and we all watch as the journalist writes it down and underlines it.

Fuji waves a cigarette around in the air before tapping out the ash into an ashtray.

'They're very well looked after. There are food rations provided each day for every prisoner, the same for every prisoner to the gram. They have their own sanatorium stocked with medicines and drugs of all kinds. They are supplied with healthful activities for mind and body, amateur dramatics and gardening, for instance. Tell them about the garden, Captain Jones.'

'I am growing vegetables,' I say.

'Yes, by the time we leave, they won't even need us.' Fuji's eyes crease up, to show just how amusing a prospect this is.

'Leave, Sir?' the journalist asks, pen hovering above the paper.

'Yes,' Fuji says, blowing smoke out over the table. 'General Kobayashi and I are returning to Tokyo shortly.'

'Who will take your place?'

Fuji waves his hand.

'Someone will be sent over in the near future.' He turns to Campbell. 'The same conditions will apply. You abide by our rules and you will continue to be well treated.'

Kob looks at the abandoned cards on the table, examining each one carefully as if they were tarot cards, our futures exposed for all to see.

'They've screwed up somewhere along the line, haven't they?' I say as we walk back to quarters afterwards. 'They're a pair of lazy bastards who are being thrown out.'

We've reached the Indian quarters. For once Campbell has nothing to say. He just keeps on walking towards his bungalow, raising a hand by way of farewell.

'See you in the morning,' I say to Elsa, and walk quickly up the stairs to my dormitory, with her voice ringing up the stairs after me: *Nos da, cariad*, as automatic as the flash bulb on that camera.

I lie in the darkness listening to five other blokes snoring around me, the corner of my blanket stuffed in my mouth, chewing mechanically. I'd looked forward to my glass of whisky tonight and I hadn't had it. Maybe I was more upset about this than anything else. I had been imagining all day how it would feel, the hit of sugar and alcohol to my brain and stomach at the same time, that full feeling only booze can give you. Those whiskies were better than a Stanley meal. They certainly kept me going for longer. It was clear from tonight's conversation that they were over indefinitely.

And then I think of Elsa, and my mother, what she'd said when I told her we were engaged to be married.

'Another cup?' She'd held the teapot up in the air for a moment before starting to pour. 'You'll have to watch her, you know.'

I don't care about anything anymore, except the fact that I didn't get my whisky tonight and there's a gnawing, gaping feeling in my stomach that I can't get used to.

But what would cross my mam's mind if she saw that photograph: Elsa, Campbell and me captured on a long exposure, playing cards with Kob and Fuji? What would she make of that single instant impressed into newsprint, blackening her fingers as she read the story underneath?

25th August

It is so hot that the entire surface of the peninsula seems to crackle in the sun. Grassy patches have worn away to yellow scorch marks, and the bouldered outcrops are hot enough to boil a pan of water.

At morning parade Fuji and Kob announce that in order to mark their final week at Stanley, they are to permit swimming. We are to take provisions for the afternoon and proceed to Tweed Bay, down the steep concrete steps leading from the hospital to the sandy beach below. We will be accompanied by a full complement of guards.

People are allowed to go down in groups of twenty or so at a time. It takes a long time to get everyone down to the beach. There is no strength left in any of us, even the children. They don't run down to the water and splash their way through the shallows, although it must be warmer than a hot bath by now. They walk, and as soon as they come across a free spot they roll themselves down to a sitting position on the sand.

One young woman walks past me, limping badly, her legs swollen with *beri beri*. A young boy has mosquito bites all over his back. Some of them have been scratched so much that they have become infected with pus and look as if they will leave permanent scars. Almost all the men look exactly the same: stick thin legs and arms, concave chests, and distended stomachs. The picnics people have brought with them look quite normal from a distance: sandwiches, cans of water and so on, but close up you can see that the lunches are made out of foul-tasting rice bread and heavily salted fish, served in tiny squares, two per person. And the cans of water are only half-full, because we have to keep some of today's cooled water for supper. In fact there will be no supper, because we all voted to bring our day's rations down here and make an afternoon of it. The best we can expect is a spoonful of rice stew before bed.

'Question,' says Campbell. He seems to be in good spirits, almost playful. I could smash his face in.

I grunt, keeping my eyes on the sand.

'When's a picnic not a picnic?'

'When it's practically a death march?' I offer, gesturing towards the limping, hobbling picnickers traipsing past us.

'He's joking,' Elsa says to Campbell. 'You are joking, aren't you?'

'How would you know?'

Liz Vernon comes over to us, her feet sinking into the soft sand.

'Elsa dear, do you want me keep an eye on Mari so you can go for a dip?'

Of all of us, Liz looks the hungriest. She's lost so much weight that what's left hangs forlornly around her wrists and ankles.

'It's all right,' Elsa says, putting Mari in my lap. 'Tommy will do it.'

Elsa's sun dress is worn through, almost transparent, like a layer of skin that has loosened and come away from her flesh, there's so little of it left. Her knees and elbows look like rocks sticking out of the shallows. The curves of her bottom are just about still visible, though, and I keep an eye on them until she is under the water and has started swimming. Campbell is quiet on the blanket next to me.

'Enjoying the view?' I say to him, shifting Mari onto the blanket so she can crawl around.

'Yes, not bad.'

He's so insipid. Makes you wonder what he'd say if he were lined up in front of a firing squad. *Yes, thanks. Not bad. So-so.* Some nights I wake up in a sweat and determine to go over there to Bungalow D with a knife from the kitchens and slit his bloody throat. Maybe I will, yet, once the garden's summer crop is over and done with.

'Ta-da, Ta-da!' Mari has found a white pebble and is waving it at me with one hand. She loses her balance and falls over. She opens her mouth to cry.

'Here you go, Mari,' Oscar says. He picks up a twig and scrapes out a pattern in the sand. 'Look, isn't it pretty?'

'Pitt-y,' Mari says. She takes the twig and scrapes her own line in the sand. 'Pitt-y.'

Elsa is swimming now. I can see her arms lifting rhythmically in and out of the water. She is moving further and further away from the land. On the beach, one of the guards is nudging his colleague and pointing.

'What's Elsa up to?' Oscar sits up and puts a hand over his eyes, scanning the horizon. 'She's too far out.'

'She'll be all right,' I say, passing another twig to Mari, who sits up on her bottom and starts drumming the earth with both of them. 'Ta-da, ta-da. Ta-da. Pitt-y.'

I pick up a handful of sand and run it through my fingers to amuse her.

'But she's such a long way out,' Campbell says again. He looks orange from top to bottom in this heat, with his hair and freckles and burned skin. Sweat is running off his forehead.

'I told you,' I say. 'She always comes back.'

'If you say so.' He leans back on the sand, but he is still peering out over the water to where her head bobs up and down.

Two of the guards are walking down the beach, kicking sand with their boots. Oscar is sitting up again.

'Elsa,' he says.

His fear is infectious. Other people are starting to look in the same direction, murmuring to each other. Children run into the water, pulling each other's arms and pointing. Mari starts to cry, not a baby's cry for milk, but a loud toddler's urgent yell, right in my face. I move away from her on the blanket, but she follows me around from corner to corner, yelling and screaming. 'Ta-da. Ta-da!' and waving a stick in my face, almost poking my eye out.

'Mari!' I say, and take the twig off her. She starts bawling then.

One of the guards has walked into the shallows. The water is over his boots and halfway up to his knees, seeping through his trousers.

'Ta-da!' Mari yells.

There is a lull in the tide, that moment where it rests on itself before turning back inland. Everything is still, apart from Elsa's dark head on the surface of the water. She must be a mile out. Behind her lies the low reach of the land on the other side of the bay. It is scrubby and wooded, with few buildings.

The guard standing in the water fires his gun straight up into the air. A few people jump and Mari stops crying.

Elsa turns and starts swimming the other way, back towards the beach, her arms rising and falling strongly and evenly.

'Thank God,' Campbell says, resting back on his elbows again.

'See?' I raise my voice so he can hear me over the din that Mari's making. 'She always comes back.'

30th August

I wake early. I know straightaway something is wrong. Afterwards I will wonder what it was that signalled trouble. Whether there had been a humming in the air that was denser than usual, or the muted sound of stems and stalks splitting, falling over themselves like a breaking wave. I pull my trousers on and head over to the garden in my bare feet.

As I come round the corner past the American quarters I see them. Greenfly. Blackfly. Pests of every description. The ripe, glowing skins of my fruit and vegetables are covered in them. I lift a cabbage leaf. The underside is spotted with eggs. I can hear them cracking open, I swear it, and the insects coming out, stretching their legs, taking a great gulp of air, and then starting to suck the sap out of every last leaf. There isn't a single plant in the entire garden that isn't withered and ruined. Bamboo poles that have fractured under the weight of falling beans poke out of the ground like chopsticks. Rows of corn that have come away from the vine are bent over. They look as if they are about to keel over completely, stalks spread out to either side of them like raised hands. Surrender. Underfoot, foliage that has acted as groundcover since the spring has either been eaten by the flies or died off in the space of a few hours.

The queue that was gathering for morning congee outside the canteen has turned to watch. Kob and Fuji appear. Fuji is grinning. Perhaps it's not the ending he expected but he evidently finds it pleasing all the same. This will make him look good back in Tokyo.

Campbell comes over.

'Bad luck, Tom,' he says.

'It's not just the veg,' I say to him. 'There's something else down there.'

'What?'

133

But Kob has already seen what's there.

'Hands above your head!'

One of the guards raises his bayonet and trains it on me.

Kob is staring at the soil between the rows of dimpled Chinese melons and dried-up pawpaws. The sun is up, blinking out a morse code on the wrought metal and wire that stick out of the ground like old bones. Kob pounces. He shouts out to the guards. They move quickly, making their way along the furrows that I first made with my clumsy bare hands. For a while all that can be heard is the scraping of shovels as they slice their way through them, turning up roots, bulbs and seeds as they go. Other guards follow them up and down, examining the earth, turning it over again in places with their fingers.

Once the first plug is found the rest seem to rise to the surface of their own accord. Cables and wires are brought up and held out at arm's length like a human sacrifice. The guards put them in the wooden crates at Kob's feet, and go back to look for more.

When they have finished, he calls me over. I start walking. Nothing else moves, apart from the sun. The prisoners, guards, Elsa, Mari, Campbell, even Mimi – their faces all have a rigid, surprised look, as if someone has brought a movie to an abrupt halt, and they are stuck in the freeze frame. I'm the only one who keeps on moving through real time. I stare at them as I pass. Mari's tiny fingers reach out to me. Her fingernails need cutting. Elsa usually does it with her own teeth because there isn't a pair of scissors small enough. Mimi's hair is a mess. Someone must have got her out of bed in a hurry to come and see this. Oscar Campbell is the biggest surprise. He looks if he's about to cry.

I stand close to Kob. He is shorter than me, and I know he hates having to look up at me.

'You were trusted,' he says.

My mouth is dry.

They march me over to the Jap headquarters and leave me with armed guards in the room where we used to play bridge. There are empty glasses on the sideboard. Through the open window I can hear a child playing outside one of the bungalows, a rubber ball smacking against concrete over and over.

By the time they come back I reckon they must be planning on taking me to Tytam Bay, where the tides are strong and southwesterly. I'll bet they're going to shoot me and leave my body to rot in the sun, then let the sea carry it away. It makes me think of the crosses we were given at Sunday school when I was a boy, made of dried-out palm leaves with points sharp as nails. We used to run down to the beach after chapel and stick them in the sand and wait for the incoming tide, thinking the water would turn them green again, but it didn't. All we woke up to the next day was a soggy mess of crosses sticking out at awkward angles, and by the following day they had been washed out to sea.

Turns out it's not the beach we're headed for, though. When we come out of the house I'm prodded in the backside and told to keep moving. We proceed along the road we call Roosevelt Avenue past the Dutch block, the ration shed and the warders' quarters, until we come to a barred gate that I've never been through before.

It is opened from the other side, so we can walk straight through it, into the prison.

September 1942

Ein Tad, yr hwn wyt yn y nefoedd
sancteiddier dy enw
deled dy deyrnas
gwneler dy ewyllys
megis yn y nef
felly ar y ddaear hefyd…

I can do most things in English, except pray.

I am in a dark room, alone. It is small. If I reach out my arms I can touch the walls on both sides. There are no windows. The door is locked. The air smells stale, as if it has only just been vacated by someone else. I wait for my eyes to adjust to the dark, but they don't. I hear nothing. I see nothing.

I guess that the blackness has a reason; to make me lose track of time. So I count, inside my head. I put a finger to my wrist and estimate the length of seconds, minutes, hours. I don't let myself sleep.

… dyro i ni heddiw
ein bara beunyddiol
a maddau i ni ein dyledion
fel y maddeuwn ninnau i'n dyledwyr…

On the second day there are noises outside my cell. People talking. Keys are jangled. I get to my feet, walk over to the door. I am swaying. I am thirsty. They shake the keys again, as if they are about to open the door. Then they walk away.

I keep counting. I am so thirsty. I run my hands down the walls. They are damp, I lick my fingers. The dirty water makes me retch.

When I am not counting, I am praying. When I'm not praying, I'm counting.

… ac nac arwain ni i brofedigaeth
eithr gwared ni rhag drwg
canys eiddot ti yw'r deyrnas…

On the third day they come to the door again. They do exactly the same as yesterday. Talk loudly and rattle a bunch of keys. I stay sitting on the floor, waiting for them to go away again. But this time they don't. They open the door and order me out.

I walk in front of them down a narrow corridor. It is all light. The door at the end is opened from the outside and then there is more light. It makes my eyes water. White concrete, white sky, white sun. The prison exercise yard. I am the only person in it, apart from the guards. They manoeuvre me out of the doorway with the butts of their guns, then retreat and close the door.

I hear footsteps behind me, but they are oddly weightless, like a child's pattering. Several of them. I turn round as they jump at me.

Dogs. Two dogs. The pet wolfhounds. They feel as high as my chest, and they are leaping, snapping at my hands and legs. I put my hands out and stumble backwards. They rip and tear the bare skin on my ankles. Their teeth sink into the flesh.

I look down and am surprised that it doesn't hurt more. It should hurt.

I hear laughing. The guards looking out of barred windows.

The pain hits just as one of the hounds, black and white with a black patch around his eye, jumps straight at my throat. I put up a hand. His bite is large, taking in my whole palm. I feel blood running down my fingers. It is warm.

They are growling, circling me, ready to charge again, when the door is opened and a voice shouts out and they run to it.

A guard comes out and gestures to me to go back inside.

I walk back along the corridor in front of him. I know which room they are taking me to because the door is wide open. I don't want to go back into the darkness. I try to memorise the light as I walk through the doorway: its reflection on the white walls, the sound of it, the feel of the day on my skin. The blood from my savaged hand is running down my leg now, dripping onto the floor. They push me into the room, but they don't shut the door. I go to the far end, turn round, and sit down against the wall. I look out of the doorway at the light. My breathing becomes slower.

Just as my eyes are about to close, there is a clap. The door is slammed shut, from the inside. All is blackness again.

I can't see anything.

A hand grabs my hair, puts a knife to my throat. I wait for the metal to cut me open. I think I want to be dead, to stop feeling my heart beating, frightened.

Then I hear a voice.

'Get up.'

It is Kob. I struggle to my feet.

The door is opened again. Two guards come in. One of them puts a blindfold over my eyes. They kick my bitten shins as we walk down the corridor.

Outside there's an engine running.

'Where am I going?' The voice feels like mine, but it doesn't sound like it.

I am dragged up onto the back of a vehicle. I am pushed into a sitting position on a hard seat.

Kob's voice comes at me over the juddering engine.

'Home,' he shouts. 'Japan!' He laughs, then taps the rear bumper twice. The vehicle pulls away.

I smell warm air, the beach, something frying in the camp canteens at the top of the hill. The green pine trees that grow between the rocks on Roosevelt Avenue.

I hear the engine gathering pace, a change in gear as we approach the long hill that leads to Aberdeen, back to Hong Kong.

In a few moments the little that I had left of Stanley is gone. The blindfold is hot around my ears. Everything is black, inside and out. I see shapes moving across my eyelids. Elsa and Mari. Then they are blotted out.

> *... a'r nerth, a'r gogoniant*
> *yn oes oesoedd*
> *Amen*

IV

Mari:
NEW QUAY, WALES, 1947

1

Mary is her English name. In Welsh, she's Mari. She doesn't have a Chinese name, she says to anyone who asks, because she is going home, and there will be no call for it. That's what her mother told her.

She is sitting up straight in the back of the car between Elsa and Tommy. The leather that presses against the skin on the back of her legs, in the gap between her pleated skirt and her woollen socks, is ice cold. She stares at her knees. They are covered in little mounds of skin that Elsa calls goosebumps.

'You'll warm up in a minute,' Elsa says, putting her hand on Mari's thighs. The soft new suede of her gloves still smells of the shop where they bought them on Savile Row before catching a train out of Paddington. Elsa had taken a long time to choose them, too long, Tommy had said. She'd set them side by side on the countertop, in different poses, first so that the right hand lay on top of the left, then side by side on the glass. They'd looked as if they were about to start playing the piano. Then she'd taken one of the two pairs, the dark red ones – *mulberry* she'd called them – and held them close to her face, the rows of covered buttons on the outside edges touching her cheek.

'I'll take these,' she'd said.

Mari had stood behind her, looking at her mother in the mirrors, reflecting on this new version of her. She was still the same as before, but paler, older, more beautiful, but a little frightening. She didn't roll up her sleeves and she didn't smile. Men looked at her as she strode down Savile Row. Even Tommy had to lengthen his stride to keep up with her, and Mari had had to run, holding both hands out in front of her, hoping that one of them would remember she was there and scoop her up and lift her along the pavement with them. But they hadn't; they'd kept on striding, talking in sharp bursts of words that sounded like marbles crashing against each other before rolling away into angry silences. She'd been glad when they'd got on the train and sat in the restaurant car, and she'd been given a glass of lemonade. She'd made herself wait two whole minutes before drinking it, her eyes on the clock above the bar, her nose over the edge of the glass, letting the tart bubbles burst against her nostrils.

She blinks away the tears. It's been a long time since they got off the train at Llandysul. She is hungry and her back hurts.

'Are we nearly there?'

'No,' says Tommy.

He has a voice that rumbles through everything around him, making it shake. Mari feels her goosebumps trembling. She turns away from him, and looks across her mother out of the window. This is like nothing she has ever known. Her mother told her it would be like flying, driving along the road between Llandysul and New Quay at night. They don't stop, for one thing. There are no buildings, no intersections, no men in uniform. There is no noise, apart from the engine of the car. The spirals of condensation on the window aren't condensation at all, but swirls of mist outside, coiled close to the ground on the ridges at each side of the narrow road. There is no moon. Above them there is nothing, and below them there is nothing, apart from the barely visible road ahead. The mist rolls towards them and away again. The car's gears screech as it struggles up Wstrws Hill, under huge bare trees whose branches reach out

144

from either side of the road, as if they might grasp the car as it passes and fling it away, down into a ditch.

'Fog's bad tonight,' the driver says, not turning round. His Welsh sounds strange to Mari, contorted into short jabs of sentences that she finds difficult to follow. She has only ever heard two people speaking Welsh – Elsa and Tommy. He has a rolled-up cigarette in his mouth. She sits forward in her seat.

'Where are we?' she asks.

'Banc Siôn Cwilt. Ever heard of it?'

She shakes her head, although when they were at Stanley her mother used to talk her through this journey at night, when she couldn't sleep, when the rats outside the window and the rasp of cockroaches inside kept her awake. But in her mother's version it was always midday, the sun high in the sky, with the thin line of sea in the distance reflecting white silver on the horizon. In her mother's story, there were foxgloves growing in the hedges, or autumn leaves at Wstrws so vivid that even the air around them was the colour of oranges. Mari hadn't known what an orange was, but it had sounded warm, and hopeful, the way Elsa said it. In the story her mother told, the sun was always out, and everything was light and shade, clearly definable.

'Once we see the sea, you'll know where you are,' Elsa had said.

But it is dark, and theirs is the only car on the road, headlights hardly penetrating the mist. The driver drops his speed as they climb the hill, until they are going at a walking pace.

'Where are we?' Mari says again, more to herself than anyone else. It feels like the empty spaces of her nightmares, when she wakes up soaked in sweat, clutching at nothing until her mother comes and she holds on to her, breathing in Elsa's sleepy smell, that warm, thick scent that gathers around her at night like a comfort blanket.

'Smugglers used to hide out up here,' says the driver. 'The mist was good for some, once.'

Mari steals a look out of the window. Shapes lurch towards the car. They burst through the fog, turning out to be trees, stunted bits of hedge, broken gates, before stepping back into the shadows of her imagination. She keeps her eyes wide open for so long that when she finally blinks her eyelids are flecked with ghosts rearing out of the soil. One of them has a face like Tommy's. Mari looks over at him, just to make sure he's still there beside her. He has his eyes shut, his shoulder slumped against the car door. She turns to her mother. Elsa sits straight, looking ahead. She has taken her gloves off and holds them in her lap, stroking them from time to time. The silence banked up inside the car is as thick as the fog outside.

In her mother's version of their homecoming there had been no Tommy.

The car bumps up and down without warning, then pitches back and fore before righting itself, throwing Mari against Tommy. He is wearing what he calls his good suit. The material is old and shiny, and it is too big for him. Elsa has folded the sleeves back on themselves, tucking the extra length inside.

'I told you I needed to hang on to it,' Tommy had said.

Elsa had smiled a smile that looked like the opposite of itself, it made her face seem so unhappy. Mari wondered why Elsa was so nice to him when he was so rude. If it had been Mari talking like that, Elsa would have told her to mind her manners.

'Sorry, must've hit a badger,' says the driver. Tommy wakes up.

'Sit back,' he says to Mari.

She pushes herself back in the seat, her knees forced flat and her shoes sticking out over the edge of the leather piping. It will leave red marks on the back of her legs, an indentation that will stay for days. When people ask her what kind of journey home they had, she will think of the red weals scored into her legs, and say nothing.

Her skirt is all rucked up, and she pulls it straight over her thighs. Her mother puts her hand on her leg and taps it gently, and Mari stops fidgeting. She puts her hands at her sides and looks straight ahead of her and counts in her head to a hundred in English, then *cant* in Welsh. When she is done she starts on Cantonese although she knows that she can only get to twenty, which is just as well, because by the time she reaches *yih-sahp* as Lin had taught her, she feels the road starting to fall away from them, under the car, so that for a moment she feels as if they really are flying, slowly coming down to earth. There are high hedges now on either side of them, but through their bare branches she catches sight of lights dotted here and there, until they get lower and lower and the lights get closer together. The car turns down a small lane, then takes a sharp left. There are houses on one side and nothing on the other. A low wall, the kind that her mother tells her to come away from otherwise she might fall, and then nothing beyond. The car stops at the first house. There is a nameplate by the door, picked out by the streetlight above. Gwelfor. She can't see the sea, but she can hear it, an angry crashing somewhere down below the stone wall.

The driver stands with the car door open, the engine still running, while Tommy counts out the notes. Most of the houses behind him are in darkness.

'Where is everyone?' Elsa says.

'Up at the hall, I expect.' The driver looks at his watch. 'Ten to midnight. Happy New Year to you!'

'Happy New Year,' Elsa and Tommy say together, as if they've been rehearsing it.

'Well,' Elsa says, as the car backs down the terrace again. 'Here we are. Home.'

And even the word itself makes Mari afraid, more afraid than she had been of the smuggler ghosts or of Tommy's black mood in the car, or of Stanley, or of Hong Kong afterwards, where even her mother said she felt a stranger after the war. She is afraid of the black hill behind the houses and the boom of the sea below. She is afraid of this place, where there are no people, no voices, no pavements.

She doesn't ask for Oscar, because she knows she's not supposed to, so she whispers his name to herself, inside her head, where no one can hear it. Oscar, Os-car, OS-CAR. But he doesn't come.

2

Elsa and Tommy start walking back down the road, the way they'd come in the car.

'Where are we going?'

Mari's shoes feel cold and hard against her feet, bumping her up and down as she tries to keep up.

'The hall,' her mother says, and then, when Mari pulls at her hand again, 'We're going to a party.'

'What, now?'

Perhaps it's always dark here. Perhaps for the people who live here, this is day.

She holds onto Elsa's hand and peers out from side to side. They turn up a steep lane with houses along one side and bushes on the other, with thorns as long as her fingers. Elsa doesn't have to tell her to keep up. The hill is so steep that Mari has to bend her legs sharply to get up it as quickly as she can, pulling Elsa with her. More houses, a crossroads, another lane, and a pool of black on the other side.

'What's that?'

'Stop asking questions, for God's sake,' Tommy spits out.

'It's all new to her, Tom, remember,' says Elsa, and then, bending over Mari, standing between her and Tommy, 'That's the playing field, where the boys play football and rugby.'

'Why is it black?'

'It's not – it's green. It just looks like that at night.'

'How do you know it's grass? How do you know it isn't sea?'

'Because I know where everything is here,' Elsa says. Her voice has an ironed-out sound to it when she is tired. 'The sea's on the other side of those houses, see, over there?' pointing towards the roofs behind them. 'Can't you hear it?'

Mari stands still for a moment. Tommy keeps on walking, but Elsa stands with her. It doesn't sound like the sea in Stanley Bay, the whisper and sigh as each long wave turned over itself and stretched out before coming to rest on the beach. It sounds like a high wind blowing, stormy, the kind of night that fills Mari's dreams with witches and parrots. Elsa starts walking again.

'There's the hall,' she says, pointing to a shape emerging from the black night up ahead. It looks like a ship from this distance. The doors are pulled tight shut, and there is no noise.

'Where's the party?' says Mari. When they'd got back to Hong Kong from Stanley there had been parties all the time, all day every day. No one had cared what she did; she was allowed to play under the table in the Gloucester, or behind the bar, or talk with the waitresses who liked her and smiled, and fold paper napkins into pretty shapes with them, and wait for Elsa and Oscar to come and find her when they were ready. She was never frightened they might forget, and they never had.

'I don't know.' Her mother hesitates, looks over at Tommy. 'It's a bit odd, isn't it?'

Tommy is walking towards the door with his big flat hand out, looking as if he will force it if need be, when it opens from the inside.

On the other side, there is nothing, at first. Only shadows. Then, as Elsa walks into the hall with Mari still holding her hand and Tommy gummed to her side, Mari blinks again and again until she starts to see shapes: the curve of a cloak, the bowed top of a trilby. There is a crowd of people facing away from her in the half-dark, looking towards a raised platform at the other end of the hall. From the stage comes a flare of light.

Mari can feel a rhythmical popping in her ears and the pulse of Elsa's hand in hers.

A figure is running down the aisle between the coats and hats. She is wearing a white, gauzy dress with a skirt shaped like a tutu, and a tiara made of silver tinsel wrapped around a circle of wire to make a halo around her head. She turns this way and that, scattering sparks of light as she moves her head. Her feet must be skipping along towards Mari on the floor, but she looks as if she is floating. She has small bones and long limbs and wide eyes. She has a silver tinselled wand that she waves to her right and left as she makes her way down the aisle, and she laughs as she sprinkles her magic dust over the coats and hats as she goes, and they turn as she passes them.

Mari is getting used to the dim light. Over the stage behind the faces there is bunting, red dragons on one side and red, white and blue stripes on the other. On the platform are hordes of children lined up in a group, the tallest at the back, and the smallest, about the same age as Mari, at the front. They have their mouths open, as if they are about to sing, or recite. Their eyes are on the white angel.

Behind the angel, a voice says from the stage, 'Ladies and Gentlemen, please give a big hand for our New Year Fairy 1947, Miss Iris Davies.'

And the room explodes with claps and shouts and whoops that burst open like firecrackers in the gaping rafters above Mari's head, and everyone leaves their seats. The women are kissing each other and the men are shaking hands and they are all saying, 'Happy New Year, Happy New Year!' until someone catches sight of Mari and Elsa and Tommy standing there, and the noise fades away. Even the fairy angel stands as still as a frozen snowdrop, staring at Mari. And Mari doesn't know who is more frightened, her or all these grown-ups, until the fairy stands over her imperiously and taps the top of her head with her wand.

'And who are you?' says the fairy.

'Mari,' she whispers.

'Mari who?'

Mari looks up at her mother.

'Jones.' Tommy's voice booms out behind her, out from the playing field, louder than everything, louder than the sea.

'Well, Mari Jones,' says the fairy. 'Happy New Year to you.'

People are saying their names and milling around them, and throwing their arms around Elsa and Tommy, and asking questions. Some of the women are taking handkerchiefs out of their handbags and patting their eyes.

'It's too much,' one of them says. 'It's just too much.'

'I know,' says Elsa. 'I'm sorry.'

Mari wonders what it is Elsa has done, but before she can ask, the arms and elbows and pinching fingers pluck her away from her mother and carry her over to a trestle table. The lights are turned up and cloths lifted from the table and Mari sees that it is covered with dishes of food. There are corned-beef sandwiches, sausage rolls, scones, cakes, milk puddings and jellies. Hands are holding out plates to her and she is taking whatever they offer her and stuffing what she can into her pockets. Someone gives her a bar of chocolate; someone else says, 'Here, have a tangerine,' and presses a soft orange round of fruit with skin on it into the palm of her hand.

'What's that?' she says, pointing to a dish that smells sweet and hot.

'Tapioca,' says the fairy angel, serving some into a bowl for her, and then, when she sees that Mari doesn't understand. 'That's frog's eyes to you, Curly.'

It looks like coconut milk with pearls floating in it. Mari puts a spoonful in her mouth, expecting the pearls to hurt her teeth but they dissolve, sticky and sweet on the roof of her mouth. The angel dollops a spoonful of jam into the middle of the bowl; the next mouthful explodes with a sharp tang of something, maybe strawberry, and a seedy grit that gathers at the back of her throat. As soon as her mouth is empty she fills it again. Her spoon feels like a shovel, and her arms get tired.

'Slow down, dear,' says a woman shaped like a rolled-up pancake with a squidgy middle.

The angel fairy is still over her shoulder, pressing a mince pie into her hand and watching her break the pastry open before it's barely in her mouth. She can feel specks of raisins and orange peel sticking to her chin.

'Eat up,' says the fairy. She never takes her eyes off Mari. She stares at her without smiling, watching the way her hand wraps itself around each mince pie and then tries to cram it whole into her mouth. Each time Mari has finished the fairy gives her another one, until a voice over her shoulder shouts out, 'Iris, come over here, please.' The angel backs away, her blackcurrant eyes still fixed to Mari's, watching her lick her lips and suck the sugar off her fingers.

Mari sits on one of the chairs and leans back against the wall. She tries to take her time but she can see food disappearing; all those children who had been on the stage are helping themselves to egg custard and sausage rolls. There is bread and dripping right next to her on the table and its suet smell fills her head. The heat circulating between the jackets and waistcoats and dresses around her gets thicker and hotter, and she looks up to ask for help, but the faces are blank again, the eyes and made-up lips all moving oddly, warped out of shape, and she can't make out what they are saying, their voices too loud and then too quiet, until she feels it again, that popping in her ears, and she creeps to the door and looks out at the black playing field and throws up, a stream of green vomit that tastes of rice that has gone off. Her mother has told her she will never have to eat rice again. Her mother is right, she thinks as the vomit forces itself up into her throat and spatters out into another puddle on the lane outside the hall, lit up only by the backs of the houses behind. Her mother is always right. But under the tang of tapioca and corned beef, she can still taste it on the back of her tongue.

3

'Frank, could you go and get some more wood from the outhouse, *calon*?'

In Gwelfor there are just the six of them, counting Nannon, Frank and the cat. Mari has made a den for herself under the table, behind the green chenille cloth that hangs over its edges. She is nursing the black-and-white cat in her arms like a baby and cuddling it. The cat holds its four paws up in the air without protest and closes its eyes.

Elsa lifts the cloth from time to time and bends down. She looks too tall, like a giant; or perhaps it's the house that's shrinking around her. Her head seems to touch the chiselled glass of the lightshade above, and everything else – the footstool in front of the fire, the gilt-edged mirror on the wall – seems reduced.

'Are you all right?'

Mari's eyelids are heavy. The air is dark and soft under the table; the sounds beyond her den are muffled by the fringed tablecloth and the red woollen rug. Her mother is holding back the tablecloth. On the other side there is a fire going under a mantelpiece with a china dog at each end. There are two easy chairs either side of the fire.

'Why the hell did he leave it open like that?'

Tommy is standing by the door, his hand on the doorknob.

'Tommy,' Elsa says.

He leans around the door, peering into the shadows behind it, as if he expects to see someone there.

155

'Tommy dear, sit yourself down,' says Nannon. 'Frank will stoke up the fire, make everything cosy for you.'

Mari tries not to stare at Nannon, but she looks so much like Elsa that it's difficult not to. But while Elsa is long and thin, Nannon is plump all over, with arms and legs that poke out almost at right angles. She has lines across her forehead, maybe because she seems to keep her eyebrows raised all the time, as if someone has just told her something she never expected to hear. Her eyes are grey like Elsa's but they are shot through with ruptured blood vessels that run in red lines across the whites of her eyeballs. She looks very tired, although she can't be, because she doesn't stop moving from one side of the room to the other, puffing up cushions to get Tommy comfortable in one of the easy chairs, then making her way straight back to the table to offer Elsa a sandwich, or a jam tart. She doesn't stop talking either, except when Tommy cuts across her.

'Shouldn't that be Franz?' he says.

Nannon puts a plate down hard on the table above Mari's head.

'No, it's Frank these days. And I'm Mrs Meyer.'

Nannon sounds as if she is pursing her lips, like someone who is on the verge of beginning a story, someone who expects everyone to listen, so Mari does.

'Frank and I got married on Christmas Day,' she says.

The burned-out remnants of the logs in the grate hiss and spark as they collapse into each other. A single flame shoots up the chimney and dies away, and the charred wood underneath starts to smoke.

'Good to get warm, isn't it?' says Frank as he walks into the room. He puts a rush basket full of chopped wood next to the fireplace and flings a couple of logs onto the fire. Each time he lifts a log, Mari sees a muscle bulging through the sleeves of his jumper. He takes a small brush with a long gold handle

156

out of a stand by the grate and brushes away the ash and specks of dirt from the slate slab underneath. When he has finished he slots the brush back into place and shifts the fire-set to one side, out of the way. It has a brass front that gleams as if it has just been polished, its smooth texture interrupted by hammered-in pictures of ships in full sail. Frank stands next to the coal bucket with his hands clasped behind his back.

Nannon walks over him. They are the same height, like the man and woman in the weathervane in Gwelfor's glass porch.

'Frank and I met at Pwllbach, like you and Elsa.'

'How lovely,' Elsa says loudly. 'Tommy, why don't you come and help yourself to a Scotch?'

'Because you can bring it to me over here.'

Elsa lets the baize-coloured cloth fall back into place and everything beyond becomes blurred and indistinct again. There is a ripple in the surface of the chenille, the clink of ice cubes hitting the side of a glass and the sound of liquid being poured over them.

Elsa has borrowed a pair of Nannon's house shoes and they are too big for her. On the way back to the table she lifts her heels, so that she looks as if she is paddling through water.

'So you were here working on the farms with the others? The Italians and Germans?' she says to Frank.

Mari would like to pull the fringed tablecloth back the way her mother had but she doesn't want them all to look at her. Through the green fronds she can see four pairs of feet: each time someone speaks, the feet move. Frank's feet shift as he answers Elsa's question. He changed his shoes to go and get the wood from the garden, as Nannon told him to; his garden shoes are old and badly mended, and a tongue lolls out from one of them.

'You didn't fancy going home at the end of the war then,' Tommy says. 'Like the rest of us.' He uncrosses his legs and crosses them again. All Mari can see is the one shoe that's still on the rug. It is a brand new shoe, bought in London when Elsa bought her gloves. The three of them all have new shoes. Mari's rub against her toes, and she takes them off whenever she can.

'You took your time, too, didn't you?' says Frank.

'There were things to sort out, after the war,' says Tommy. He says it as if there had been a mess in Hong Kong, and he, Elsa, Oscar and Lin had all set to and tidied up the place, until everything was just the way it had been before. Mari doesn't remember it like that. Everything was old or broken, it was true, but there were smiles on faces and plenty to eat. She didn't know what it was like before, in any case. All she knew before that was Stanley, the slow pendulum of night and day, and waiting for something to end, and when she asked her mother what, her mother saying, 'The war,' and waving her hand out around her, taking in the turquoise sweep of Stanley Peninsula, the low hills and crags the colour of uncooked dough, and the water's edge at Stanley beach, which shone white in the morning sun.

Nannon steps into the centre of the room. She is wearing a pair of sandals that would be better suited to a hot summer's day in Stanley, worn without socks as they clambered down from the compound to the beach where they were allowed to swim, while the guards watched. But she's wearing them with nylons to keep warm, and her toenails look as brown as thick coffee.

'I think we should have a toast,' Elsa says. 'New Year, new beginnings.'

'You needn't worry.' Nannon sounds agitated, as if her eyebrows are flitting up and down again. 'We're moving into the flat above Bristol House. You three must stay here. Together.'

'Yes, we haven't had much time together, have we, Elsa?' says Tommy.

He sounds as if he is sitting forward in his chair. Mari listens as a fizzy liquid bubbles into glasses above her head.

'Since I came back from the dead.'

'Oh no, we never thought you were dead, either of you, did we Franz… Frank? We never gave up.' Nannon rocks her heavy frame back and fore on her ugly toes. They look like the knobbly, undersized potatoes they used to grow in Stanley. Elsa used to make Mari collect them in a basket with ancient newspaper folded over the hole in the bottom so they wouldn't lose even one.

'To Elsa and Tommy and Mari, and the happy times ahead,' Nannon says.

There is a chink of glasses from by the fire, hesitant and out of time with each other.

'And to Nannon and Frank, and a long and happy marriage,' says Elsa quickly. 'And as for moving out, I won't hear of it, not into that pokey little flat. There's plenty of room for us all here.'

The woollen loops of the rug press comfortably into Mari's cheek. Nannon's voice is fluttering up and down like someone playing loose scales on the piano at one of the parties Elsa and Oscar went to at the Gloucester Hotel; when she reaches the crescendo of the story, Mari is jolted back to herself; then comes a polite ripple of laughter from Elsa and a 'Ha!' from Frank, and Mari tumbles back down into a sleepy pool of inner silence again, absorbing unconnected fragments of the conversation. From time to time she hears a pecking sound like a bird tapping its beak against a window, and she sneaks a look out from under the tassels and watches Elsa's fingers picking away at the surface of the tablecloth.

Mari lies back on the rug, feeling her shape imprinted deep into it next to the cat, like the hollowed-out dent a body leaves in the sand. They lie curled up facing each other. She remembers swimming with the other children on the beach at Stanley, the sand that was made up of all colours – brown, gold, white – and letting it slip through her fingers grain by grain, watching as they caught the light. Usually, instead of swimming, Mari had spent her allotted half-hour sitting in the sand. It was because she was hungry, Elsa had said. They were all so weak because there wasn't enough food; there weren't even enough of the potatoes that pushed their way through the earth in the tennis courts. Elsa had said to Oscar, 'Look at that. Poor Tommy's potatoes,' and Mari had said, 'Who's Tommy?' and Elsa had told her to go and play with the other children. She wonders where they are, all the other children, if they are asleep behind stringy ferns made of green chenille, if they've been eating bread-and-butter pudding while people look them up and down, saying 'And who have we got here?'

The voices recede into swishing murmurings, someone saying 'It's getting hot,' and pulling the sash up, and the voices becoming indistinct from the swell of the sea below, until they are gone and there is only Mari and the loops that press into the side of her face as she lies washed up on the rug, abandoned.

4

Her mother promised her it would get light, and it does, eventually, but it is the noise that wakes her first. Not the sea, although there is that too, but a heavy clopping sound coming up Lewis Terrace. It knocks unevenly as it comes up the rise from Water Street, getting louder and louder until it is right under her window, making the glass shake in its frame.

'The milk cart's here,' she hears Nannon calling around the house.

Mari sits up in bed, her heart beating fast, shivering as the cold air reaches her skin. She hauls herself up and out of bed, tripping over a fold in the rugs. She holds one hand out against the window frame to steady herself. Just underneath the bay window, a horse and cart have come to a halt outside Gwelfor's porch. The horse has a brown mane and a head that shakes back and fore from time to time. It is huge, with a dark coat almost hidden by a blanket that has been flung over its back and tied round its middle. Spokes of hot breath spurt out of its nostrils. It is attached by a pair of reins to a shallow cart with two high wheels, and a metal and brass urn inside.

Mari pulls on a jumper over her night dress and a pair of long socks, and runs downstairs.

Nannon is by the hat stand, poking around in a drawer.

'Where's my purse got to?'

She looks up and sees Mari.

'You're up already, there's a good girl,' she says. 'Ah, there it is.'

She takes Mari's hand.

'Come with me.' She is smiling, as if something nice is about to happen.

The kitchen is full of steam. Clothes hanging off a Sheila's maid above the range are sending out a warm soapy scent mixed with the smell of percolated coffee coming from a metal jug on one of the rings. Nannon reaches out to a low, open shelf under the dresser and pulls out an earthenware crock.

'There,' she says, nestling it in the crook of her arm. 'And for you, this will do.' She passes a yellow mug over to Mari.

Mari grips the mug tightly as Nannon whirls her out to the hall and opens the door to the porch. The cold hits her straightaway, and the frozen slate slabs of the floor of the porch hurt the soles of her feet through her socks. The porch has double doors onto the street glazed with coloured leaded glass, a purple tulip dotted with green tips the shape of diamonds. She sees the horse's rheumy eye looking at her from the other side, shaded green by the stained glass.

'Whip these on,' says Nannon, pointing to a pair of her own shoes. Mari slips into them and stands behind Nannon as she opens the double doors of the porch.

'Morning, Siôn,' Nannon says to the man who is standing holding the horse's reins.

'Cold one this morning,' the man says, clapping his hands and stamping his feet, making the horse shake his head again. 'Isn't it?'

They both stand and look over the top of the milk cart at the sea. Mari tries to see through the spokes of the red wheels that stand higher than her head. The cold runs through her body and she shakes involuntarily, like the horse.

'What's it to be?' says the man.

Nannon holds the big crock out and says, 'I'll have a quart,' and the man turns to the cart, leaving the horse's reins to dangle in mid-air. He reaches out for one of the metal containers that hang off the long hooks at the back of the cart, and takes one of the hand cans. He heaves himself up into the cart and hunkers down in front of the churn, turning the key until the milk hits the bottom of the can. He swings himself back down, holding the can in one hand, and pours it into the dish Nannon is holding. The milk steams out of the crock.

'Still warm, that is,' he says, looking at Mari. The skin on his eyelids and nose is red and shiny and looks as if it hurts in the cold. He is wearing gloves without fingers that show the blistered skin on the back of his hands and a ring of dirt around each nail. He winks at Mari and says to Nannon, 'And what will the little lady be having?'

'This is my niece, Mari, back from Hong Kong.'

'Hong Kong, is it?'

The man takes a good look at her. He has watery, deep-set brown eyes like the horse.

'Could you let her have half a pint in the mug? I'll give you a ticket extra,' Nannon says.

'No need for the little lady from Hong Kong to give me a ticket. This is my present to you. A welcome home present.' One of his runny eyes blinks over and over, as if he can't help it.

'You are kind. I'm much obliged to you,' says Nannon.

He lifts Mari up above the gold-framed paraffin lamps onto the high cart and although she doesn't like the feel of his hands on her through her jumper she doesn't say anything. He lets her turn the churn key herself and sit on the low bench against the cart's curved back and drink her milk. She drains it almost in one gulp, looking at the trees that poke up above the low wall from the houses below and the sea beyond them, layer of grey on grey.

The man lifts her down again and she says thank you, and he gives her a smile that creases his face up into a crackled glaze.

163

'*Croeso.*'

The horse flicks its tail. The man pats its haunch lightly and they move along up the road to Hedd y Môr next door.

Nannon says, 'Quick, quick, let's get you into the warm,' and they go back inside. With the rest of the house still asleep and the fire in the range heating her through, Mari sits at the kitchen table, running her fingers over its lined surface, waiting for her breakfast.

5

Nannon's good moods seem to dissipate with the cold of the early mornings. Some days she leaves early to go over to Bristol House; but often she stays in Gwelfor and works her way through a list of tasks she has written up on a piece of slate in the pantry, ticking them off in chalk. As she becomes absorbed in the day's work she withdraws into herself, as if she can only concentrate if she is absolutely quiet, and if Mari talks to her or asks a question she shakes her head, or waves her away. After breakfast she wraps Mari up in layers of old jumpers and a heavy coat, puts a cheese sandwich packed in baking parchment in one pocket and an apple in the other, and walks her to the front door.

'Where's Mammy?' Mari asks. She isn't used to being away from her mother. She is used to the safe enclosure of the barbed-wire fence at Stanley. If her mother told her to go off and play she meant for her to run around the exercise yard with the other children brandishing a broken bit of wood and a ball made of paper and glue, with Elsa's shadow in one of the workshops behind her, tall against the window, singing hymns in Welsh that no one apart from Mari could understand, and the man from the quarters down close to the beach, Colonel Jackson his name was, who had a false leg and said that hearing '*Calon Lân*' so far from home made him cry.

But Nannon says, 'Your mam and dad need to rest. We need to let them sleep on a bit.' And Mari learns that once the leaded porch doors are closed behind her she must get moving, or her fingers and toes will start seizing up in the cold, and she must keep moving and not come back until lunchtime, otherwise Nannon will just send her out again. She looks up at the end of Lewis Terrace, where the road rises sharply off the end of the village so that it looks as if it leads into the sky, and then she glances the other way, down towards the end of the stone pier that curls out and away from the boat sheds on the slipway. The still water has a smooth surface the colour of fresh cream, broken up in places by pale milky lines of tide trails.

From Gwelfor the place is all chimney pots, made up of three terraces cut through with lanes that run down from the brow of the hill. Mari finds that whichever way she chooses sooner or later she will end up at the shoreline below. She puts an arm out and grasps the metal rail that has been riven into the wall. She listens. There is a scraping sound coming from somewhere, but the acoustics here are refracted by the sea, the walls, the side of the hill.

When Mari walks down from Gwelfor, she has to brace herself, stretch out with her head leaning backwards and her feet poking away from her, to stop herself from going down too quickly and tripping over her own feet. Everything changes and shifts around her with each elongated step she takes. The grey of the sea deepens. The houses seem to move with her. There is a small patch of light over to the west, over the water below the shallow cliffs, as if there is a sun somewhere behind the clouds.

As the mornings get lighter, Mari starts to look forward to her walks. She is glad to escape the kitchen table in Gwelfor, watching Nannon, Frank, Elsa and Tommy passing each other the marmalade without being asked. The hedgerows start to send out feathers of light green leaves, and the stream running parallel with Water Street thaws out: Mari can hear it rushing down the terrace to meet the sea. The desperate sound of hungry seagulls is softened by the burbling of the wood-pigeons in the trees behind Gwelfor. On these milder days, she can only hear the sea once she is right above it.

She sees a red fishing boat coming into harbour from behind the pier, its wake a wrinkle on the surface of the water. There is a rock on the beach that looks like a broken-backed whale, its skin scored through with lines like paper cuts. It sits in a ridge of shattered shells that have been pounded against the back of the pier by the tide and trapped between the rock and the base of the wall.

The rocky pier is built in two layers: the top level, where Mari has come to a halt, has benches dug into its thick walls, and the next level has uneven ladders of steps cut into it, which means that you can move from one to the other as you please, although there is nothing to hold on to apart from the slippery stair above. Nannon has said they are treacherous and Mari mustn't go and get herself killed on them. The stone is dark and wet and too cold to sit on.

Mari turns and looks back at the village from the end of the jetty, and at the patterns of children's footprints in the sand on the beach. Nannon says that she must go to school. Elsa says they must give Mari time to get settled. 'Elsa,' Nannon says. 'It's been weeks.' Mari is afraid of the school building, its bricks wet and oily like the seals who dry themselves off on the rocks down by Cwmtydu. She is nervous about the cruel fairy angel from the party, who has a name, but she can't remember it. She dreads being on her own with her in the school, having to go to the toilets which she has seen are the other side of the yard. Every time her mother asks her if she wants to play with other children, like she did at Stanley, she shakes her head.

The scratching sound reaches her again, coming at her from the slipway between the boatsheds and the rocks overhanging the beach. It is a sharp metallic noise, rhythmical and relentless. She lowers herself down the steps, using her hands to stop herself from slipping.

'Ha, ha, ha!'

It's a man's laugh, ricocheting against the sides of one of the upturned boats on the slipway.

'You're right, there, boy.'

The slipway is stacked with lobster pots made of metal and rope. There are tufts of sea plants sticking out of some of them, drying off. They have a mysterious series of inner nets like cobwebs. Boats are turned on their bellies so that they look like the broken-backed rock on Penpolion, propped up off the ground by neatly stacked towers of splints and bricks and tyres. They look funny with their hulls up, emptied out somehow.

'Hello. Who's this, then? Elsa's girl, isn't it?'

There is a man behind one of the upside-down boats, its hull white and smooth like the underbellies of the gulls that wheel around in the sky above them. He has tiny feet and a tiny head, but an enormous middle with trousers that hang off a belt made of blue twine. He has pulled his hat down over his forehead but it doesn't hide his nose, which is shaped like a cauliflower. Behind him is another man, facing away from Mari, who is rubbing down the tip of the hull with a metal scraper. Flecks of red paint are flying out in all directions.

Mari slips out of sight.

It is high tide; water reaches her feet in an upwards rush. Metal clangs against metal as the swell lifts the circular hooks embedded in the harbour wall. She listens to the rustle of the water and stares over the bay towards the cliffs on the other side, lined with trees that look as if they are about to fall onto the rocks below.

There is a car coming in on the new road behind the collapsing row of trees above Traethgwyn. The sound of its engine travels across the water, and Mari sees a man standing at the top of the pier turn his head. There is a bang as the car engine backfires, and the man jumps and puts his hand out against the wall behind him. His face has no expression on it; neither frightened nor angry. It is a tired, dead face and she hates it. It is Tommy's.

'Hey,' the man with the scraper shouts out to his mate. 'Ossie, have you seen who's up there?'

'Well, I never. Tommy, mun!'

Tommy must be able to hear the man with the purple sprouting nose, but he looks as if he hasn't. His head is still cocked in the direction of Traethgwyn, scanning the line of trees as if he is expecting another shot to come from there.

Mari is embarrassed. He does this all the time, ignores people when they are speaking to him, and Nannon says it is very rude, whatever you've been through. Her words pierce the dark of the unanswered questions in Mari's head like the gleaming red and emerald buoys on the surface of the water, or strung up outside the houses in nets.

'Tommy, boy. What you up to?' shouts the man.

Mari doesn't dare look up again. The surface of the slipway under her feet has been washed over by the sea so many times that it looks as if the tide has become fossilised, its swirls worn into the stone.

'Bloody hell, what's got into him?'

The man has turned back to the boat and started scraping again. The other man says something, too low for Mari to catch. She glances over her shoulder at Tommy, the ungainly way he climbs down, his body rocking from side to side, his big trowel-shaped hands trying to find a purchase somewhere on the wet rocks. He looks as if he might fall into the water below, but he doesn't. Mari is afraid he might catch up with her, so she turns and runs through the mess of ropes, wires and bits of wood that fill the spaces between the boats, She darts her way in and out of the upturned hulls, between the men, and runs all the way up the hill so that by the time she reaches Gwelfor her heart is beating out of time with the rest of her and she has to stand in the porch to catch her breath before raising the latch and going in.

'Look at you.'

Her mother's voice is amused, not angry. She doesn't tell Mari not to come close to the bath, or to mind she doesn't get wet. She smiles as Mari tugs at her cable-knit jumper, pulling her elbows up inside the sleeves, lifting it off over her head.

'Want to warm up?' Elsa says.

Mari's clothes smell of seaweed and have bits of dried paint stuck to them. She pushes them to one side with her bare heel. Elsa doesn't say anything, like Nannon would, about learning to fold clothes away properly, or not making a mess for other people to clear up. Elsa is lying back in the bath with her head resting on one end of it, the enamel lip making a hard pillow for her head. She closes her eyes and stretches out, her toes almost touching the faucet at the other end. Then she gives a little sigh and pulls herself up in the water, bending her knees.

'In you get.'

Elsa stands up to help Mari over the side of the bath. Her hair looks long when it is wet, plastered to her shoulders. Unlike Nannon, who looks fatter without her clothes – Mari has seen her, walking back to her bedroom with her dressing gown not done up, gaping to reveal an expanse of stomach and breasts that sway to and fro – Elsa looks even thinner. The bones on her wrists and ankles stick out, and the skin on her stomach hangs down, as if there used to be more of her, like the rolls of crepe that Nannon has for sale in Bristol House in all colours: bruised purple, lemon yellow, the blood-red of crushed raspberries. She holds Mari's hands as she gets into the bath and then they sit down together, as if they are counting to the same beat, like children on folk-dancing night up at the Memorial Hall. Elsa lets Mari's hands drop at just the right moment, when she's sitting in the water with it coming up to her chin.

Elsa sits down, her breasts white as meringue, one nipple bigger than the other, the pale pink scar across her stomach wide like a smile.

'What's that?'

Mari points at the pink line as it reddens under the water.

Elsa lays her hand over it.

'It's where you came from.'

She turns sideways and props her thin legs over the side of the bath, leaving space for Mari.

'Tommy says we come from Pwllbach.'

Mari tries the word out for size again in her head. It feels like a word she isn't supposed to say, like 'Oscar'.

Water drips out of the tap and echoes round the bathroom. Drops of condensation roll down the plain white tiles and into the bath, pocking the surface of the water.

'Well,' said Elsa. 'Yes, that's where he's from. It's a farm. It's only up the road, near Capel y Wig. It's where his mam and dad live.'

'He says it's where I'm from,' says Mari.

'Does he?' Elsa has propped her head against the edge of the bath and closed her eyes again.

'I want to see it,' Mari says. 'Why do Tommy and Frank go all the time, without us?'

'To help out on the farm. They're busy lambing,' says Elsa. 'You'll see it soon enough. We're going there on Sunday, after chapel.'

She doesn't speak to Mari any more after that, and Mari sits pulling her knees into her chest, feeling too hot, sweat gathering around the roots of her hair, but not wanting to say so, looking at the shape of her mother swelling under the water, becoming enormous, so that in the end there is no room for Mari, and she says, 'I want to get out.' Elsa sighs and lifts herself up again and helps Mari over the edge of the bath before clambering out herself. She reaches for a towel, looking out though the frosted glass of the window at the garden behind, although you can't see anything apart from the shapes made by the sheets as they blow about in the wind, taking too long to dry. Nannon and Elsa will bring them in and hang them on the pulleys in the pantry and leave them there for a day or so. By the time they are put back on the beds they will smell of Nannon's baking, and Mari will wrap herself up in them and close her eyes and dream of sweets and fluffy rice crackers that dissolve against the roof of her mouth, and Lin, who gave her fortune cookies and told her she was a lucky baby, lucky for everyone and beautiful too, and stroked her hair.

'Can I write a letter?'

Mari has seen the postman delivering up and down Lewis Terrace, after the milkman has done his morning round. You can hear him whistling from the kitchen. Elsa says, 'Anything?' as Nannon comes back into the kitchen, and Nannon says 'No,' putting the lid on the butter dish and carrying it out to the cool shelf in the pantry.

'Who do you want to write a letter to?' Elsa is silhouetted like a black paper cut-out against the light from the window.

'Lin,' Mari whispers.

'Of course you can. She'll be waiting to hear from you.'

Elsa bends down and wraps a towel tightly around Mari, her fingers deft and light, as if she has done this a thousand times before, although they didn't have any towels in Stanley: they used to dry themselves on scratchy brown blankets that had rough, chewed edges. She puts her hands on Mari's shoulders, and says, 'Come on, let's get you dressed so we can make some lunch before Nannon comes home.'

6

Mari is walking with Frank, behind Tommy and Elsa and Nannon. The hill is steep, and her legs are tired, and she's glad when Frank takes her hand without waiting for her to ask. He doesn't make her rush, and he answers all her questions, although sometimes he is quiet for a while before the answer comes.

'What are those?' she says, pointing to a row of dead moles strung up on a fence, their pink forepaws pointing to the sky. 'Why are they there?'

'They're trouble for farmers this time of year. They're a nuisance, digging up the earth.'

'Like tigers,' says Mari.

'Tigers?'

Frank looks down at her. He has dark circles round his eyes that bunch up when he smiles.

'Yes,' she says. 'There was a tiger at Stanley, as big as you, and the soldiers had to hunt it down and shoot it, and they carried it round the camp for us to see.'

'Did it make you frightened?'

'No,' she says. 'It made me hungry.' They had been standing in rows in the assembly yard. The tiger was tied upside-down to two poles and carried around the camp. Its orange-and-black fur was matted in places, and she could see the muscular surface of its skin underneath.

'Did they give it to you to eat?'

'No.' She shakes her head. 'Mammy says they gave it to a Japanese general in Hong Kong.'

'Are you hungry now?'

'Yes.'

'We're nearly there,' says Frank, squeezing her hand and starting to walk more quickly. 'Perhaps Sara will have made something good for us to eat. Maybe a tiger sandwich or two.'

She looks up at him quickly.

'Are you telling the truth?'

'No.' He smiles again, his hand firm in hers. 'Just my little joke.'

'That's nice, to hear you laughing,' Nannon says. 'Is Uncle Frank making you laugh?'

Mari laughs again, because she likes the way Nannon is looking at Frank without saying anything while she walks between them, sheltered by their smiles. The hedges on either side of the lane are as tall as trees, broken up by banks of red and yellow primroses and purple pansies too high up for Mari to pick them, and in any case, everyone is walking quickly now, as if they've just remembered they have somewhere they need to be, and don't want to be late.

Suddenly the hedges come to a stop, and they are surrounded by grey walls on all sides, and a yard full of mud turned over into slimy humps by hooves and boots. The buildings are joined together around three sides of a square, with their roofs at different levels. Windows and doors seem to have been put in anywhere, uneven and haphazard; the effect is what Nannon would call hotch potch. Through an open doorway into the barn, Mari can see rolls of damp, rotting straw that have been caught in the rain. A dank smell hangs over everything. There is rusting metal strewn around the barn's open doors – tractors without wheels, trailers with broken catches, a car with a door missing, listing to one side.

'*Mawredd*,' Elsa says. 'What's all this?' She looks at Frank.

'Glyn won't let us shift anything,' Frank says, 'I've offered, many times…'

He pauses.

'The war sent him mad, quite frankly,' Nannon says quickly, as if she's tired of waiting for someone else to say it. 'Well, you must have seen that, Tommy.'

'He's just getting on a bit,' Tommy says. He's looking over at the farmhouse at the far end of the *buarth*. Mari sees the corner of a curtain being lifted, and a pair of eyes peering out, black as moles.

'Oh, come on,' says Nannon. 'You've seen for yourself what he's like, what's going on here. Frank can't do anything about it, it's not his place, but you can.'

A woman's voice shouts over from the other side of the *buarth*.

'Are you just going to stand there all day or are you going to come in? Where've you been? I've been expecting you for half an hour.'

Mari jumps. The face from the window is at the door of the farmhouse.

'It was Mr Pendry's fault,' says Nannon. 'There was an awful lot of sin to get through at Towyn this morning.'

The woman's face softens into a nest of wrinkles as she walks over to them, her heavy boots wading through the mud, her hands out towards Mari. She is wearing a grey scarf wrapped around her hair anyhow, and an apron tied loosely over her droopy breasts. The roses on her apron have hardly any colour left in them, and there is a splash of something, gravy or soup perhaps, across the front.

The woman grips Mari's hands, but her fingers are greasy and she smells of lard that has been used for cooking and left to settle in the pan and then used again, until it stinks of burned gristle. Mari pulls away.

'Funny little thing,' the woman says. 'You're never six years old.' She looks cross.

'Yes, I am.'

'Mari,' Elsa says.

'That hair of yours, it's a mess, all over the place.' And then to Elsa, 'You should cut it.'

'We like it just as it is, Sara,' Nannon says, her voice more polite than Mari has ever heard it.

'Well, you'd better come in,' says Sara. 'Glyn's up in Cae Melyn, planting. He'll be back shortly.'

She takes them round to the back of the farmhouse. Inside it is dark and too hot. Mari blinks, trying to get her bearings, but there is only one window, the size of Tommy's hand, and the fire throws a pale light over everything, giving the room a shape, but no definition. The bubbled-up paper on the wall looks wet.

'Come and sit down,' Sara says, pulling Mari towards the fire.

Mari takes her coat off as Sara presses her down on a wooden settle with a high back. Sara pushes Tommy down next to her, but he only stays still for a moment before getting up again. He makes his way through the smoky air towards a door that leads out into a passage. The door is open. Tommy stands by it for a moment, like a hare about to leap up on his hind legs. Then he dives towards it and slams it shut. No one says anything, but Mari sees Sara looking at him, her black eyes glistening. Tommy comes back towards the settle and sits back between Mari and Elsa. Nannon and Frank sit at a low bench next to a trestle table.

There are two plates on the table, one loaded up with sandwiches, and the other one with a fruit loaf. It has already been cut into, and looks dry, apart from the glacé cherries.

Sara goes over to a dresser that fills the wall next to the window. It isn't like Nannon's dresser at home, decorated with tea services dipped in gold lacquer, and a doll from the Galapagos Islands made out of shells, and a wooden figurine from Japan with one hand bent up to hold her pointed hat straight on her head. Sara's dresser is laid with mismatching, chipped plates banged down any old how, and bundles of letters stuffed behind other bundles.

Sara sits down on a chair with a high, spoked back next to the dresser. She groans with relief, as if she's forgotten that the rest of them are there.

The back door opens and an old man comes in. He is holding a stick and wearing a cap flat on his head. His body bends over the stick like a crumpled-up piece of paper.

'*Shw mae*,' he says.

Everyone murmurs in return, apart from Mari. It's like being in chapel and not knowing what to say, and sitting there feeling stupid while everyone else speaks together, looking at the wall above the *seiat*. The fire is making her hot and dizzy and she's tempted to make a run for it out into the *buarth* while the door is open. Sara gets up slowly, leaning one hand against the arm of the chair.

The man shuts the door and takes off his coat before sitting down in an armchair close to the fire with a shiny patch on the back. Elsa and Nannon start moving around the room with Sara, slicing into the *bara brith*, pouring hot water into the teapot and letting it draw, taking plates and cups round to the men before sitting down themselves to eat.

'*Diolch*,' Frank says.

'You took your time,' Sara says, settling down in her chair again.

Mari wonders who she's talking to, but everyone else turns to Elsa. She seems young, sitting back on the low settle with her legs bent up. She looks as if she would bolt too if someone opened the door.

177

'Well?' Sara says.

Frank reaches out to the cake dish.

'This is good, Sara. Mind if I have some more?'

Sara nods, a sour look on her face.

Nannon draws herself up to the table.

'Don't you like Frank sharing your kitchen, Sara? After everything he's done for you? Keeping the place going?'

Glyn coughs, sending a spittled arc of crumbs and chewed fruit over Mari.

Nannon turns to him.

'Why are you all being like this to my sister? She's home isn't she? She and Tommy are here aren't they? Together? With Frank and me.'

'Oh yes, indeed,' says Sara. 'No wonder I don't come down to the village no more. Bloody Germans making themselves at home. And you.' She points at Elsa. Glyn is staring into the fire, chewing his food painfully, as if even the cherries hurt his teeth. 'Fashion plate. Some help you are. Poor Tommy.'

Sara sniffs loudly, ending with a snort.

Mari puts her plate down on the shelf next to the grate, spilling crumbs. She gets up, relief running through her as she moves away from the heat of the fire. She walks past everyone, straight to the table. She turns the sandwiches over first, tipping the bread and butter and loosely cut ham onto the floor, and then she up-ends the plate holding the *bara brith*, sinking her fist into it as it rolls over and hits the table, pummelling at it until its dry surface breaks, scattering fruit and crumbs over the tablecloth. She turns to Sara, stares into her moleskin eyes, and says in English, 'I don't want you to be my *mam-gu*.'

She runs to the back door and fiddles with the latch until it opens and she sloshes her way around the muddy *buarth*, first this way and that, not quite sure where to go, and then she runs away from the noise of pigs squealing into the barn, deep

178

into the bales of straw, and hides behind one of them, under a row of curved sickles hanging on the far wall. A pair of heavy shoes is coming towards her, making a sucking, slurping noise as they are drawn in and out of the wet mud. They reach the slate floor of the barn, their heavy heels hardly muffled by the wisps of straw that lie everywhere.

They come to a halt. Mari stays crouched down, waiting. Tommy lifts her up onto one of the bales and turns her over onto her front and smacks her backside.

All the way home, Mari remembers not to complain, although her bottom is still sore. She walks behind the rest of them, the hedges getting taller and darker to either side of her. They reach the brow of the hill and the sea comes into view, unsteady on the horizon, with the houses swaying, reflected in the darkening water.

There are no stars and no moon. The others walk ahead of her, shoulders bent, not looking back.

7

They don't go to Pwllbach again after that, not all together. Tommy and Frank leave early in the morning to milk the cows before breakfast, and if Mari is up early she sits in the kitchen watching Frank binding his feet with strips of cotton before he puts his hard-toed boots on; '*Fußlappen*,' he says to her, putting one hand on the top of her head, before going out the back way, letting the door bang shut behind him. But Elsa and Nannon stay in New Quay, and Mari stays with them. She gets used to having breakfast on the scarred kitchen table in Gwelfor, then lunch in the back kitchen at Bristol House, when Nannon has turned the sign from 'Open' to 'Closed' saying, 'You'll get junket for pudding today if you eat your greens.'

At first it is enough to follow Nannon around, picking up offcuts of material from the floor, using her magnet to collect pins that have spilled out over the counter, turning trims of lace back on their cardboard rolls. If Mari happens to look up out of the window and see children going by on their way to school, she hides behind the counter where Nannon keeps her paper patterns until their whistles and catcalls have moved on down the road.

Nannon moves the mannequin to one side and puts a table in the big bay window. She brings out her sewing machine and her tailor's belt and lays the belt to the right of the machine. That's where it should always be, she tells Mari. She says that before she can even let Mari touch the machine she needs to learn about cutting. She gives Mari a piece of chalk and a pair of sharp scissors and tells her to draw shapes on old bits of material. Mari likes the feel of the scissor handles, the sound the material makes as it gives way under the sharpened blades. She cuts out starfish in plain calico, pigs made of sprigged cotton, mustard pods of herringbone gorse. As she gets better at it, Nannon lets her use the pinking shears. She chops out waves with jagged tops through reams of old linen.

'Good,' says Nannon, looking at her handiwork over her glasses. 'We'll be able to move on to stitching next.' Mari wants to use the sewing machine, but Nannon says that must wait until she's learned how to do things by hand, so Mari practises making patchwork pieces, hexagons tacked onto firm paper, then sewn to each other.

When she has spent weeks being a good girl, and more weeks doing as she has been told, she is allowed to thread the machine and turn the wheel by its handle, listening to it clacking as it goes, ignoring the women's voices as they pass the shop window on their way to the butcher's. She only looks up once they have gone, her hand on the wheel. Bristol House is the highest house in the village, says Nannon, with the worst view. The bay is almost completely blocked out by the houses below, apart from a gap where the road turns down into Picton Terrace. There's a block of dark-blue sea the size of Mari's patchwork pieces, and the backs of houses, and the butcher's more or less opposite. She can see straight into the back of the butcher's, past the umbrella stand and ceramic tiles, through to the glass-fronted cabinet behind the counter.

After lunch Mari watches from her sewing table as Henry the butcher stands at the window making sure that the blind is rolled all the way up, and the sign on the door turned from 'Closed' to 'Open'. Women go past Bristol House holding empty baskets and string bags. Mari sees them crowding into the butcher's, picking over the rabbits piled up on a tray, not skinned yet. One of the women puts a hand out and squeezes their kidneys, one after the other, until their eyes pop open. Mari can see the women's mouths moving through the glass, and Henry taking their tickets and money and slamming the till shut. The tray holding the rabbits shakes, and they look as if they are dreaming violent dreams that almost wake them up, making them shudder before they settle back down again. Henry's red fingers reach out for them one by one and he skins them on the chopping board on the counter. By the time the women pass under Mari's window again all that will be left in Henry's shop will be an untidy mound of grey fur.

But today there is an interruption. Mari knows the sound of the van before she sees it, the racket it makes as it struggles up the hill, the choke pulling back before the driver puts his foot down one more time in an attempt to reach the top. It is full and heavy today, she knows that from listening to Nannon and Elsa chatting over breakfast. It's on its way down from Pwllbach with slaughtered lambs in the back, their testicles cut off, according to Nannon – 'to make them sweeter,' she said to Elsa, pulling a face. People have been waiting weeks for this delivery, Nannon said. 'There's going to be a riot, I tell you.' Not a *rabbit riot*, though, Mari thinks. She likes the sound of the words, rubbed up against each other like that.

The exhaust backfires as Glyn parks outside Henry's, obscuring the women and their rabbit riot. Frank is sitting next to him, the window wound down, his elbow resting on its frame. He sees her and Nannon look out at him and he gives them a little salute.

'I don't think I can bear to watch those women elbowing each other out of the way to get at my Frank,' Nannon says. 'I'm going to put the kettle on.'

But Mari stays where she is, watching as Frank gets out and opens the back of the van. He carries the lambs' carcasses wrapped in newspaper, oozing blood onto the pavement. Glyn is sitting completely still in the driver's seat, his eyes straight ahead of him. When Nannon comes back, Mari asks her what he's thinking about and she says straightaway, 'Nothing at all. When it's light Glyn gets up and goes out and does the milking and sees to the fields and closes gates and mends fences. When it gets dark he goes back to the house and has something to eat and goes to bed. That way there's nothing for him to think about, not a single thing.'

'What do they do with the balls?' Mari asks.

'What balls?'

There is a shout from just under the window. Mari gets down from her chair and looks over the frame of the sash. Underneath, on the other side of the glass, is a boy a bit bigger than her, crouched over his marbles in the gutter.

Nannon comes up behind her, her shadow throwing Mari's view of the boy into a crescent of darkness.

She raps on the window.

'What are you doing down there?' she says. 'Go away. You're making my shopfront look untidy.'

The boy stands up. He has a scarf wrapped round his neck, even though it's too warm for a coat. Nannon keeps her eye on him.

'Shouldn't you be at school?' she says.

'Sore throat,' the boy says through the glass. He does a mime for her and Mari, cupping his hands around his neck as if he is about to strangle himself, then pointing at his Adam's apple, muffled in the layers of his scarf.

'Go on, then,' Nannon says. 'Off you go.'

The boy picks up his marbles and moves down the road, towards the butcher's. The bell above Henry's door rings again, loudly, and Mari sees Frank coming out. He gets into the van, taking his time while Glyn starts the engine.

They move slowly along the top of Hill Street, towards Mari's window. The boy is standing between her and the van. Next to Glyn, Frank looks even more animated than usual, as if he is talking to himself, continuing some conversation that he'd started with Henry. His lips move and his eyes roll around; he looks as if he's weighing up some news Henry had put out on the chopping board for him to sample, chewing things over. Then he catches sight of the boy, standing almost in the path of the van, and his expression changes. He reaches out for the driving wheel, putting his arms across Glyn's, steering it away from the boy, just as the boy throws his marbles at him, each one ricocheting off the van's rusty bonnet with a crack before rolling back into the gutter under Mari's window.

'Bloody Jerry!' the boy shouts, as the van swerves past him, picking up speed. He stretches his arm out above his head and holds his fist in a ball above his head.

Nannon knocks on the window furiously.

'Get inside, right now! Or I'll be having words with Eluned.'

The boy goose-steps through the door of the porch next to Bristol House, his right fist still raised.

By the end of the afternoon, rain is beating against the shop window. When Mari is tidying up her things, she sees the boy again. He is bent down on his knees on the street outside, his hands out in front of him, his face turned away from the wind and rain coming off the sea, picking up his marbles one by one.

Mari taps on the window, quietly, so Nannon doesn't hear. The boy comes right up to the glass, frowning.

'They's lambs' balls, they are,' she said.

'Damn, bloody damn you, you bugger,' the boy shouts, so that Nannon comes. When she sees the boy, she says, 'Oh don't you mind Richard. His mother didn't want him back after the

184

war, so poor Eluned is stuck with him, and she won't put him in the home in Carmarthen.'

'What home?' Mari says. She's hungry, but she doesn't want to think about supper, in case it makes her think about lambs' balls diced up with gravy on her plate, how they might stick in her throat.

'The children's home,' says Nannon, banging drawers shut and putting her reels of coloured cotton thread away in their basket. 'Come along now.'

Mari gets up off her chair and turns away from the window without looking up, because she can sense that the boy is still there on the other side of the glass, and she doesn't want to see the look on his face.

8

The post office smells of beeswax and adhesive. There is wood everywhere, set in panels the length and breadth of the walls, and the counter is higher than Mari's head. There is someone on the other side though, she knows that, because she can hear the muted banging sound of a rubber stamp.

Elsa pulls her forward. There are two people in front of them. A woman stands at the counter, whispering instructions about a delivery to Shrewsbury. The man behind her is the man from the boat on the quay, with the trousers held up with twine. When he sees the woman at the head of the queue struggling to lift a parcel onto the counter, he reaches out and picks it up by its knotted string.

'Here, let me help you.'

A woman in blue-and-red uniform comes out from the other side, lifting a hinged stretch of the counter and doubling it back on itself. She takes the parcel back round to the other side and closes the counter again, disappearing from view.

'Hot for the time of year, isn't it?' says the woman at the head of the queue. 'At least it brings in the holidaymakers.' She turns round, either to include Elsa and Mari, or to make sure they aren't the people she's talking about. 'Mind you, you can't move on the beach for their picnics and their blankets and their towels.'

Elsa bends down to Mari and says, 'That's where we're

going, afterwards. You can have a swim and an ice cream if you like.'

Mari shakes her head. She doesn't want to go to the beach.

'That's me all done, then, for today,' says the woman with the parcel, gathering up her purse and bank book. 'Many thanks, Sheila.'

She walks past Mari and Elsa towards the door. As it opens it lets in a sliver of midday sun, and voices from the shop next door. Mari is wearing a poplin blouse with short sleeves, and she can feel the skin on her forearms tingling in the heat.

It is almost their turn.

'It's money I'm wanting from you today, Sheila,' the man in front says.

'Well, I'll give you what I've got, Alun, but I'm running a bit short.'

'Can you give me ten, by any chance?'

Mari doesn't hear her reply but it must be what the man wanted because he gives a satisfied grunt and leans on the counter, waiting. The room falls silent as the postmistress sets to counting her way through a bankroll, licking her thumb and forefinger, crisping up the new notes between them as she counts them out loud, too quickly for Mari to follow.

As he opens the door out onto the street a streak of blind heat hits the back of Mari's neck, and she steps out of it, forward with her mother, right up to the counter, even though it means that her nose is almost pressed into the wood.

Elsa takes the letter out of her bag.

'Pop it on the scales,' the woman says.

Mari cranes her neck as Elsa puts the letter onto the scales above her. It is face down, with the address facing the wrong way round. She pulls on Elsa's arm. Elsa ignores her.

'Where's it going to?' the woman's voice sounds distant, as if she's moved away to get something.

'Inland.' Mari loves her mother's voice. When Elsa speaks, people move in closer to her, put their heads on one side, and listen. Except this woman.

'Where to?' the woman's voice sounds impatient now.

'London,' Elsa says.

'Pass it over.'

Elsa takes it off the scales and holds it between her fingers, as if she doesn't quite know what to do with it. It is still upside-down, and Mari can make out the address for herself.

'R-A-C-S-O,' she says out loud, spelling out the letters.

'Quiet, please, Mari,' Elsa says, the smooth depths of her voice lifting sharply, making her sound like Nannon. Mari runs her fingers over the wood panelling in front of her, examining the grain of it, the contours of lakes and countries and oceans and bottomless pools all petrified into its surface. But when she puts out her fingers to touch the wood it is impossible to get a grip on it. It feels flat and smooth, and her fingers slip off it.

'You must be feeling quite settled now,' the woman says. 'Back to normal.'

'Yes, thank you, Sheila.'

'Is it a nice area of London?'

'What?'

'Clap-ham,' The woman's voice sounds as if she's reading it off a piece of paper.

'I wouldn't know,' says Elsa. 'I haven't been there.' And then quickly, as if she's just remembered, she opens her bag. 'I've got another one, for Hong Kong. How much will that be, airmail?' she says, reaching out Mari's letter to Lin, written on paper that was see-through and rustled like tissue paper, and was hard to write on.

'Don't worry,' Elsa had said, when Mari's pencil had made a hole in it. 'Lin will understand.'

Mari had been sitting on Elsa's knee drawing a picture for Lin, while Elsa wrote her own letter, dipping her fountain pen into a pot of ink, then writing without hesitating, in one drawn-out rush. When she'd finished the letter and held it down against the blotter, she sat still for a moment, hugging Mari. Mari carried on drawing her picture for Lin, a pretend photograph of her, Elsa and Oscar sitting on the beach at Stanley, her playing with a twig making shapes on the surface of the sand, while Elsa sat up on her knees, and Oscar stretched back on his elbows, his long legs crossed at the toes.

'Can I have a pet bunny?' Mari said, her eyes still on her picture.

'Certainly not,' said Elsa. 'Frank would skin it, and Nannon would put it in a pot.'

Elsa's breath felt warm against her ear. Mari watched as she took her letter off the blotter, folded it up carefully and sealed it in an envelope. Underneath, on the blotter, the words took a long time to dry off. They looked odd, the wrong way round.

'All my love,' she says out loud, and then, when nobody says anything. 'All my love.'

Sheila's head pokes out from above the counter.

'You're a sweet little girl, aren't you? Mind you, not so little any more, is she?'

Mari looks down at her shoes, tight on her feet.

'No school for you yet, then?' Sheila's voice comes at Mari again.

'She's starting after Whitsun,' Elsa says.

Sheila comes out from behind the counter to lock up after them. 'Early closing today,' she says to Mari. 'I'm off down the beach like everyone else.'

By the time Elsa and Mari have been back to Gwelfor and collected their things and settled down on the rocks off the end of the pier, they see Sheila sitting alone in the middle of

189

the beach, surrounded by clusters of women and children. A group of boys are making a racket, racing each other, wincing as the balls of their feet hit the burning sand,

'Fancy a dip?' Elsa says to Mari, in the water already. 'I'll hold you tight.'

But Mari shakes her head and stays put on the rocks while Elsa dives under and disappears for a long time before popping up, spraying out water like a dolphin. She dives under and swims away again for too long. Mari is afraid to count in case she reaches a hundred and Elsa isn't there, at the surface of the water. Instead she keeps her eyes on the rocks, on the tightly bunched limpets that grip to their edges, like paper cocktail umbrellas bleached of their colour until all that is left are their paper-brown spindles, clinging to the rock for dear life.

9

Mari can hear voices in the kitchen from the porch. She takes off her shoes and puts them into the top of Frank's wellingtons, where no one will see them. She knows the door won't make a noise, not if she's careful, nor the hinges either, because Frank is good at keeping things in order. He spends his Sunday afternoons on odd jobs for Nannon, buffing up the door knocker, oiling hinges, fixing bits of fence at the top of the orchard. She stands on the striped red-and-white runner in the hall and holds her breath.

'And I told him,' she hears Nannon say from the other side of the kitchen door. 'He'd better get his act together, or people will start to take notice. People will talk.'

'Does it matter?' Elsa's voice sounds sharp. It's not the voice she uses to talk to Mari.

'Yes, of course it matters.' Nannon sounds irritated too. 'He should be looking for another posting. Thinking about what to do next. How to keep you, and Mari.'

Elsa doesn't answer. One of them is slicing vegetables, wet metal tapping against the wooden chopping board over and over.

Mari walks up the stairs on the tips of her toes, avoiding the tread five steps up that she knows will creak if she puts her full weight on it, making sure that she doesn't stub a toe against the stair rods. As she reaches the top she can feel water still dripping off the bottom of her hair at the back but she doesn't

191

look round to see if it's left a damp patch on the carpet. She crosses the landing to her bedroom, and slips in as quietly as she can, closing the door behind her, turning the china knob with its painted yellow roses all the way round, until the catch is shut. The bed looks perfect, as it always does. Nannon changes the sheets every week, and puts the fresh set on herself, pressing out the starched corners, smoothing them away to each side. 'There, that's better, isn't it?' she always says to Mari.

Mari pulls the covers back and climbs straight in. Her wet hair will soak through the clean pillow case, but she just wants to burrow down under the weight of the blankets, even though it's the middle of the morning and she's not supposed to be here. Elsa took her to school after breakfast and isn't expecting her home until lunchtime.

Although the sky on the other side of the sash window is a sharp blue, pretty to look at, she closes her eyes, and does what she always does when she's trying not to cry. She makes a picture in her head of Hong Kong, as if she is drawing it in pencil, and tries to colour it in mentally, from edge to edge, until she's happy with every detail. It's getting more difficult each time, though. There is so much she can't remember now, about Stanley, and Hong Kong afterwards. It is only her mother's repeated telling of certain stories when she asks for them that confirms them in her memory. Even then she's not sure she's connecting the stories in the right way, putting them in the correct order, manipulating them like sand patties into the necessary ending, adding water, moulding them between her fingers until the loose yellow grains of sand turn dark and cling to each other, making the right shapes. The End. For that's what everyone in New Quay has been saying to her and Elsa and Tommy: that their story has such a happy ending. Who would have thought it, people say to them? That after everything you would find each other and come home, after

Elsa waited for you in Hong Kong all that time, never giving up (looking at Tommy), refusing to believe you were dead. How wonderful. 'Yes, better than the movies,' Tommy says.

The problem is that if Mari wants to remember the last day she saw Oscar, she has to call to mind the day she first met Tommy, for they were one and the same, beginning and end.

They'd been sitting around in what was left of the American Club. No one was out on the terrace, because of the monsoons. Rain and wind battered against the French doors, and the room filled up with people who'd come in to shelter from the weather, and found themselves sitting down, having a drink, and making an afternoon of it. All around them the moisture on people's clothes was drying off, and the air felt steamy and thick. Elsa was sitting on one side of Mari, and Lin on the other.

'Are you bored, Mari?' Oscar bent over to her from time to time.

'No,' she said. And it was true. Although she was having to sit still in the middle of a room of grown-ups, there was so much to look at that she hadn't seen before, and so much to think about – the looks on people's faces, their animated voices. Besides, they had eaten a large lunch, and she'd even been given a hot chocolate afterwards when she'd asked for one, and she was leaning in against her mother, feeling milky and sleepy. And there was a lull in the conversation, and Mari closed her eyes. She was looking forward to going back to the apartment with Elsa and Oscar, to rolling herself up in a ball between them in bed, and waking in the morning with their hands and arms all tangled around each other, like the frocks and shirts and blouses that lay around the room, breathing out the smell of her mother's perfume. Elsa's dressing table stood up against the wall behind, its pots of cold cream and jars of lavender water with their lids on crooked and their tops not quite screwed on. The base of the blind knocked gently against the window frame behind them. Oscar's back was up against Mari's face. She could see his freckles through his vest if she put her fingers out and stretched the cotton to make it transparent. He stirred, and she turned over, back towards her mother. Elsa opened her arms in her sleep and pulled Mari into her chest. One breast had slipped out of her negligee. Mari put her thumb in her mouth and the nail of her forefinger on the soft hairs around the large pink nipple. She stroked her finger backwards and forwards, as if Elsa's breast was a toy rabbit, or a teddy.

But when Mari opened her eyes again, she wasn't at home in bed with Elsa and Oscar. She was still in her chair at the American Club, with its covering ripped, and some of its foam gouged out, by the Japanese, Lin said, who were gone now, and there was Tommy staring into her face, his big, thick fingers holding her hair.

At first he'd smiled, as if he knew her.

'She's got my curls,' he said, but then he'd turned away, rubbing the back of his hand against his eyes. Elsa and Oscar had stood up. Lin came over to Mari, took her hand and said, 'Come with me, little one,' and took her off to the bar next door, and sat her down on an old settee and played with her while she peeped through the cracks in the partition into the lounge, spying on the fragments she could see of Elsa, Oscar and Tommy, and listening out for the broken bits of words that were being thrown around between them. *What the hell – how were we to – my wife – my – expect – here I am.* Elsa's grey eyes full of tears. Lin saying, 'Look, look!' dropping folded paper flowers into a cup of water and holding Mari's hand as they opened out into perfect crimson circles dotted with yellow stamens and green paper leaves. This was what happened, every time, Lin said. They never refused to open. The water made it happen.

Mari tries to connect the fragments, to tell herself the story that will make a paper flower of a happy ending, but she can't. Her head feels cold and wet against the stiff pillow case. She remembers listening to the voices behind the partition getting louder, while the rain ran in trails down the windowpane, until Oscar got up and came over to her, and told her that he wouldn't be seeing her for a little while. And she had pushed him away because she was tired and had been upset by the man who'd tugged her hair and she wanted her mother, and then Oscar was gone.

At least, that's the way she remembers it today, as she watches the seagulls diving into their nests on the chimney tops of the houses beneath, their cries ripping through the sky. They fly off again, down towards the sea, but still she can hear a baby gull that hasn't learned to fly, walking up and down Lewis Terrace, its constant screaming tearing through the day, until Mari thinks that there is nothing else, only this chafing ache inside her head that will never go away, scratching her eyes from the inside, pushing the tears out.

She cries at last, loudly, until she hears a knife clanging against the quarry tiles in the kitchen, and footsteps chasing each other up the stairs, and they come into the room, Nannon first and then Elsa.

'What's the matter?' Nannon sounds cross, angry that something has happened and she didn't see it coming, Mari can tell. She's wondering how Mari got into her bed and stayed there so long, her wet hair soaking the clean clothes, without Nannon knowing anything about it.

Elsa puts a hand out to stroke her head.

'Are you ill? Did they send you home?'

Mari shakes her head, still bawling, trying to drown out the baby gull outside.

Nannon puts a hand to her hair too.

'What in God's name?' she says. She brings her face close to Mari's and sniffs.

'Is that what I think it is?'

She looks at Elsa.

'What happened?' Nannon says.

Elsa puts a hand on Nannon's arm and Mari sees that Elsa knows already what happened: she's guessed that the smell from Mari's head is the stench of the water in the toilet at the school, that is in a black-bricked building on the other side of the yard, with 'Girls' painted on one side and 'Boys' on the other. Even though she had gone into the girls' side, Richard had followed her in with Iris and they had ducked her head in the fetid water with brown bits floating around in it and held her under until she'd had to open her mouth and let it in and swallow a mouthful of it. Only then had they lifted her head up and laughed as she had run off, out of the school gate and all the way up to Lewis Terrace, thinking to herself, *This is how it ends.*

'I'm not going back to school,' she says.

'Well you've got to go somewhere,' Nannon flashes back. 'Come on, out of that filthy bed with you, and let's get your hair washed and the sheets changed.'

'Where?' Mari says, as Nannon and Elsa pull at the sheets, as if they are pulling against each other.

'Somewhere, I said,' says Nannon.

'Nannon,' Elsa's voice cuts in. 'Not yet.'

Nannon clears her throat. 'Well now, that's enough nonsense for one day.'

Elsa says she has a headache and goes to lie down. Nannon takes Mari to the bathroom to wash her hair, using her own special mixture of egg yolk and vinegar to condition it. Afterwards she lets Mari eat her sandwiches in the rocking chair in the kitchen with the cat, until her hair's dry and she can go and put her shoes on and walk down to the end of the pier and back before tea.

10

Elsa and Nannon have let her close all the doors and have the hallway to herself. In Gwelfor and Bristol House there is a long thin passage running the length of the houses from front to back. Even though the houses themselves are different shapes, the hallways are the same, with smooth black-and-white tiles, and mottled glass in the porch doors.

It is Sunday afternoon, and they are all at Bristol House because Nannon wants to measure Elsa for a new summer dress once lunch is over and done with. Elsa and Nannon are washing up in the kitchen, the clink of china plates through the door softened by tea towels and cloths. In the parlour to the other side of the passage are Tommy and Frank, not talking, just sitting. Tommy will be smoking and reading the paper. He spends a lot of time reading the paper, although he must read very slowly because he never turns the pages, at least not when Mari has her eye to the keyhole.

Frank is always doing things. Once he's had his one cigarette he will be up and out into the tiny back yard making a pot holder out of bits of wood, or glueing the lid of the sugar bowl back together so that you would hardly notice the cracks in its blue-and-white spotted surface. Nannon says that he can't help himself. She smiles as she says it.

He is always finding things too. This morning, while they were in chapel, he went walking on the beach and came back with an empty tea chest, and a rubber ball. He put the chest out in the shed in the tiny yard at the back, and he gave the ball to Mari, telling her to keep it to herself.

Her fingers had wrapped themselves around the ball, although her hand was just too small for it. She rolls it up and down the hallway, listening to the smooth noise it makes as it rolls from one end to the other before bouncing softly against the two doors, first the front and then the back.

Someone turns the kitchen doorknob from the other side. Mari runs after the ball, catching it with one hand and holding it behind her back. Elsa comes out, carrying a tray with two teacups and a plain brown teapot and a small jug on it.

'The children next door are playing in the yard, if you want to go outside,' she says. The cups tremble in their saucers. Mari shakes her head. She runs to open the door for her mother. Elsa smiles at her and disappears into the sitting room, pushing the door shut with her foot behind her.

Mari wants to roll the ball again, but she waits for Elsa to come out, her face flushed and a smile still fixed on her face that disappears as she turns back to the kitchen. Mari can hear the children next door screaming at each other in the back garden. A swing made out of a plank and some rope hangs from the small apple tree and they are fighting over whose turn it is to have a go. The little girl squeals. Mari is glad that she doesn't have a brother, or a sister, for that matter, or a boy staying in the house like Richard, whose mother didn't want him back after the war because she is too poor and she's got five other children. This is all hers: the neat tiles, the lines of the walls, the framed cross stitch on the wall. A small, high table stands on thin legs next to the back door. Mari can't see into the pot painted with parrots and fronds of grass that stands on a doily on the top but she knows that this is where Frank puts his watch, to keep it safe, checking the clasp on its silver case to make sure it's shut before putting it in gently, in case it might break the porcelain.

Mari tiptoes from one end of the hall to the other, counting the squares as she goes until she reaches the front door. The glass panels aren't as pretty as the ones at Gwelfor, they are just a plain arrangement of two colours, but they are rich colours all the same, blue and mulberry. A dark shape moves across the leaded glass, throwing a shadow into the hall. She lifts the letterbox, although she knows already who it is. His long shadow looks too big for his body, like Rumpelstiltskin's. He has a peaked cap, baggy trousers, a pouched bag hanging off a long strap, two nets, one large, one small, and a long-handled hammer that he carries over one shoulder. And even though it is hot, he is wearing gloves, big, thick gloves.

It is the rat catcher. For no reason, it seems, there are rats everywhere. They play hide-and-seek behind the Memorial Hall; they race after the dustcart like children playing; they trickle along the streets in the dusty gap between the pavement and the road. They appear out of the drains that come out of the sea wall. Nannon says it is the heat.

It has got hotter and hotter and so has the rat catcher, running around, wiping away the sweat as he chases after them. He hits them over the head through his nets with the hammer, leaving muddied patches of blood that don't wash away in the rain because there hasn't been any. Children come across claws and bits of flesh and poke at them with dusty sticks, waiting for them to move, and screaming when they imagine that they do.

Mari lets the letterbox fall with a clatter, and the rat catcher's mulberry shadow gradually disappears, like blood leaching away.

The door from the parlour opens behind her.

'Coming to watch us chop wood?' Frank says.

She follows him and Tommy out into the yard. It is tiny, with a brick wall behind. The boy next door is sitting high in an apple tree. He stares down at them.

Frank takes the loose branches he's brought down from Pwllbach. He sets them on a large thick ring of tree trunk, and starts splicing them one by one with hard, swift blows. He grunts as they fall open. Tommy leans back against the gate and blows smoke out through his nose, tapping the ash off the tip of his cigarette over and over. The boy, Richard, is throwing fistfuls of grit at Frank, but Frank swats them away. They leave red marks on the back of his neck. Tommy rubs his cigarette out under his shoe, and starts to load the chopped logs into the shed to dry. Their insides smell sweet and juicy, like grass.

Mari looks up at Richard. He puts his tongue out at her and throws another handful of grit at the back of Frank's head.

She turns on her heel and goes indoors, into the kitchen. The kitchen still smells of the pork loin that they had for lunch, although Elsa and Nannon have been busy washing and wiping everything down. Elsa opens the window, the top half down in the sash, to let some air in.

'There, that's better,' she says.

'Shall we get started, then?' says Nannon.

'Oh, I don't know if I can be bothered. I can manage with what I've got.'

'No you can't, and you've got a stack of coupons going to waste. Come on, let me measure you up. Come into the shop.'

So the three of them troop into the shop and no one says to Mari that she's not supposed to be there. It is shady and cool because the blinds are drawn. She feels like her mother's shadow and she likes it. Elsa stands in front of the mirror.

'No need to be shy with me,' Nannon says. And Elsa starts to take her clothes off, slowly, until she is standing there in her underwear. She stares at herself, as if she is looking at someone else. Nannon turns to her basket to get her tape measure and Mari sees the tremor in her hands. Nannon puts the tape measure against Elsa's shoulders, and she says brightly, 'How about a nice long skirt dress with a big belt, straight across the shoulder. Full in the skirt, you know? They're all wearing it.' She points in the direction of the illustrated magazines spread open on the counter.

Elsa says nothing, still looking at herself in the long mirror. A dull thudding noise comes from the garden outside, like someone banging on a locked door in a fury.

'It's only the kids next door playing with old tennis balls, take no notice,' Nannon says. 'That lad is a nuisance. The sooner he gets taken away, the better.'

'Is she going to go through with it?' Elsa asks.

'Poor Eluned. She's got a kind heart, but she's had enough.'

Nannon measures Elsa's chest, her fingers knocking against her hollow ribcage. She holds the tape loosely so it won't press into Elsa's skin, as if she's afraid it will leave a mark. She tots up the inches from the nape of Elsa's neck to just under her knee, while Mari counts the bones that stick out all over, like the stringers of a half-built hull.

Nannon, for once, doesn't fill the silence with words. Mari closes her eyes and breathes in the smell of Nannon's love that clings all about her: the scent of dried egg and braised liver on her apron, lavender water around her cleavage, the soft mass of her overheated flesh under her plain cotton dress, the care in her fingertips on Elsa's skin.

Then there is a scream from outside and the sound of tennis balls falling to the floor, and a girl crying. Mari opens her eyes. She runs to the back porch. The jamb of the door is swollen and cracked, and she has to pull the handle hard to open it.

Tommy is standing with the axe raised, blood dripping off it, pieces of sawn wood on the ground all around him. On the trunk they've been using to split the logs is a rat, its head separated from its body.

Mari hears Elsa and Nannon coming up behind her, but she can't turn round. She can't stop looking at the rat's red eyes, its headless torso still twitching, its worm-pink tail. Tommy and Frank are staring at it too. Frank has one hand at his neck over the little red marks, as if they've started itching. The yard next door is empty.

Mari stands in between them – Frank, Nannon, Elsa and Tommy – feeling the end of the afternoon closing in all around them like the hot bricks of the garden wall.

11

Mari knows the names of all the months now, in Welsh as well as English. Sometimes she gets them mixed up, although she can't see how that can be her fault, for there seems to be nothing about 'July' that might make it the same as *'Gorffennaf'*. *'Gorffennaf'* – the end of the summer – seems the wrong word to Mari, anyway, for when July arrives it isn't the end of the summer at all, far from it. Come August, there are still holidaymakers everywhere, promenading up and down the pier in black jackets. They strip down to their bathing suits and lay out bath towels and blankets on the hard, baked sand of the beach below. Heat blisters out of their uncovered skin, and in the evenings the scent of calamine lotion attracts the midges.

And in August there is the regatta – bunting and fancy sundresses on show, and a warm breeze smelling of tar and candyfloss blowing through the crowds. Mari sits on her knees near the lifeboat shed eating wilting cucumber sandwiches from a wicker hamper and watching the races. Boats run stern to stern and people's cries carry on the wind as the damp sand under Mari's feet dries into crinkles that burn the skin between her toes. Elsa and Nannon drink tots of a brown sugary liquid out of egg cups, until they laugh at the way the bay winds out around them, and sit back against the warm smooth cliff-face jutting out from the sand, and fall asleep with their hats over their faces and their skirts hitched up. Mari sits up straight as a mast on the blanket, waving the wasps away from the abandoned egg cups, making sure that she doesn't fall asleep too before the tide comes in.

She doesn't want August to end, because August keeps her close to Elsa and Nannon, and August keeps Tommy at a distance, busy with Frank up at Pwllbach rolling up hay into bales, or lending a hand on other farms in return for help with their own. She doesn't want August to be over just yet, because when it is there will only be four weeks left before she is sent away to school in Cardiff.

Nannon takes her into the shop on a Sunday afternoon, and makes her up a new night gown with her initals stitched into it: MJ – she doesn't want it getting mixed up with the other girls' clothes in the laundry, Nannon says. She tells Mari about the department stores in Cardiff, says that she and Elsa will take the train and visit Mari and go shopping. Often. And Mari will spend the holidays at home.

When Nannon says the word 'home' Mari finds herself trying hard to catch her breath, like the day when Tommy had smacked her, but she doesn't ask any more questions. She has been afraid to, ever since she heard Tommy and Frank and Elsa and Nannon talking about Kenya behind the kitchen door. She'd opened the door and gone in and they'd fallen silent. She hadn't known what *Kenya* was, if it was English or Welsh, like July or *Gorffennaf*, so she'd looked it up in one of the encyclopaedias in the parlour. She'd put her fingers to the photographs of savannas covered in acacia trees with fluffy, feathered tops that looked like an old woman's hair, and then she'd closed the book, and shut her eyes, and tried to conjure up what she could of Stanley, an afternoon spent with Elsa and Oscar sitting on the hill above the cemetery, playing noughts and crosses in the earth. But although Oscar was still there in her mind's eye, marking out an X in the sand with a stick, he was as indeterminately monochrome as the zebras and leopards in the reference book, his eyes a washed-out tint that looked like no colour at all.

Perhaps as she gets bigger, she thinks, as July turns into August and then September, life will become greyer and less distinct, until she won't remember the smudged-out features of Oscar's face at all.

But when August does come to an end Mari finds it isn't that simple: after a light covering of frost like finely bobinned crochet across the terraced lawns, the days heat up rapidly, and the blues and greens of the bay below become brutally sharp. Nannon calls it *haf bach Mihangel*. An Indian summer. More words that sound nothing like themselves. All Mari knows is that it isn't time to leave yet.

Elsa and Nannon are making sloe gin. They stand in the kitchen pricking the sloes with silver needles. They've set everything out first so they can get them bottled up before lunch. On one side of the low sink is the pyramid of purple-blue fruit they carried home with Mari along the new road the day before. The bloom on their skins looks mildewed, but it's better that way than to pick them too early, Nannon had said, her fingers pecking like beaks in and out of the bushes, slinging handfuls of sloes into her basket without stopping, until she said she needed a breather and reached for her thermos flask. Although the sloes will never be sweet, she told Mari, as they sat on the grass verge taking long gulps of tepid tea from the same cup, at least the first frost has bitten into the sour edge that lies just under their skins.

Mari pushes her head up from the table by her elbows. On the other side of the draining board, set out on an old tea cloth, are three empty bottles and a heap of sugar in a covered bowl. Nannon starts pushing the sloes into the empty bottles. Elsa has lit the range, and the room is filled with the scent of ginger tea and woodsmoke.

'No dozing at this time of day,' says Nannon, nudging Mari's head gently out of her hands. She goes to fetch a basket from the scullery and comes back in and puts it on the table.

'Damsons,' she says. 'Up in the orchard. I want you to strip the two big bushes of them before they get too ripe and start falling off.'

Mari hardly ever goes into the back garden that falls in dug-out terraces to the back door. Usually it is hidden from view by clothes drying in the wind. Frank has put in two washing lines running from the top to bottom of the garden, and the pegged-up sheets hang down at sharp angles. She knows where the orchard is, though, through the gate and behind the air-raid shelter.

'What did you need a shelter for here?' Tommy had asked when he'd seen it.

'Swansea was bombed and half-burned out, wasn't it?' Nannon answered without hesitating. 'They said all ports were vulnerable, even here.' She'd turned to Elsa. 'You could see the glow in the sky from Pwllbach.'

They don't need the shelter now, Elsa tells Mari, but it is still there between her and the orchard, a bank of earth and corrugated iron with a gaping mouth that makes it look like Twm Siôn Cati's cave. It scares her. This is the reason she doesn't like going out into the garden. She doesn't like having to go past that silent hump of dead soil, with the outlines of ghosts moving about in the sheets behind, half-formed shapes that stutter in the wind like a broken news reel.

She tries to pretend it isn't there as she pushes the dripping sheets out of the way to get up to the orchard.

'Hello.' Tommy is sitting under an apple tree, his hair made wild by the breeze, his face fuller now that he's been eating Nannon's food, his eyes bulging.

She sets to picking damsons off the bush, some of which have started falling already, just as Nannon said. They have burst open on the grass underfoot and lie face-up, their yellow insides grimacing at Mari like Sara's jaundiced smiles. Mari doesn't want to go to Pwllbach again. And she doesn't want to get another hiding from Tommy. She puts the basket down and carries on collecting the damsons. They are a deep purple, deeper than the sloes, almost black and they are big too, so that she can only pick them one by one.

Tommy gets up and helps her, his hands moving quickly, his blunt fingers holding the damsons as carefully as she does, making sure they reach the bottom of the basket without being spoiled.

When the basket is full he takes it off her and puts it down on the grass at the base of the apple tree before sitting down again.

'Come and sit next to me,' he says, patting the mossy patch next to him.

They look out over the roofs of Lewis Terrace. Mari's bottom is starting to feel damp through her skirt, and she tries to lever herself up onto one of the apple tree's protruding roots.

'You can see all the way up to Snowdon today,' Tommy says. 'It's a shame I didn't bring the binoculars out with me.'

Mari wonders if he means that she should run and get them. She makes as if to get up off the ground, but Tommy puts out one of his big hands and rests it on her arm until she sits back against the tree trunk again. She looks straight ahead, at the distant houses painted in strong reds and yellows on the promontory of Aberaeron, then to the north, at Llanon, a low topple of cottages and a church as small as the miniature heads of cow parsley that she cuts up to make bouquets for her dolls' house. Last of all there is the long seafront at Aberystwyth, with the peaks of Snowdonia beyond.

It is cold in the shade of the tree and she wishes she'd put her jumper on to come out instead of skipping away, pretending she couldn't hear Elsa's voice carrying up into the garden from the scullery behind her.

'What does she write in those letters?' Tommy says lightly, as if the answer doesn't matter at all.

'I don't know.'

'How do you think we can find out?'

'I'm going away to school.'

'Maybe not. Maybe not if you can help me find out what she writes about.'

'How?'

'Next time she sends you to the post office, you come and see me. You bring me the letter.'

'And then I won't have to go away?'

'No.'

'Promise. Do you promise?'

'Yes, I promise.'

Mari looks out over the sea. She feels sorry for the boy who lives next door to Bristol House, Richard, because he has to go to the orphanage in Carmarthen next week, and there's nothing he can do to stop it. He doesn't whistle when he delivers the papers any more; instead he flings the *Cambrian News* into the porch so hard that it hits the bottom of the front door with a thwack.

Tommy takes his hand away from her wrist and she gets to her feet.

'Will you do it?'

'Yes.'

She takes the basket and starts to pick her way down the path between the sheets hung out to dry.

The soles of her shoes are still wet from the orchard. She knows she's going to fall before it happens. She doesn't trip;

she just slithers off one of the slate steps and lands on her knees in the back yard. She sees the basket dropping from her hands and rolling down to the back of the house, with damsons flying out of it. Some of them land on the kitchen window, leaving marks on the panes. She wonders why Elsa doesn't come away from the sink and open the back door to see if she's all right. Still on her knees, she looks through the smeared glass at her mother. But Elsa isn't rinsing or pricking sloes or stirring them into the gin; she is bent over, clutching her sides and retching into the basin while Nannon stands at her side with her arm around her, pulling Elsa in close, looking straight ahead over Mari's head, taking no notice of the split open ugly faces of the damsons against the grass.

12

Nannon and Elsa are in a strange mood, fussing around the leftovers on the breakfast table, and looking up at the clock above the range again and again. Nannon says they will take the car to Lampeter, and when Elsa asks about the petrol coupons she says the petrol coupons can go to hell for one day.

'Am I coming?' Mari asks.

'What?' Nannon says. She is busy taking a wad of notes out of a jug on the dresser and counting them. She puts some of them in her purse and the rest back in the jug. 'Yes, yes, of course. You can go and put your coat on, if you've finished your toast.'

Mari runs to the coat hooks in the hall, wiping her mouth with the back of her hand. She waits on the road outside for a long time, while Elsa and Nannon get themselves ready. She can hear a wireless crackling in one of the houses further up the terrace, and someone shouting down on the quay, although when she leans over the wall she can't see anything apart from the roofs below and the navy of the sea.

When Nannon and Elsa come out of the house wearing lipstick and sunglasses, they look like photographs of themselves. Nannon sits in the driver's seat, with Elsa next to her, and Mari behind. Mari could lie lengthways if she wanted to and fall asleep, but she doesn't feel sleepy, so she sits up and looks out of the window.

Nannon waves a gloved hand at a woman standing on the corner of Lewis Terrace and Water Street. The woman gapes

211

through the window. 'Going somewhere for the day, are you?' she calls out.

'Yes, that's right,' Nannon beams back at her.

The woman opens her mouth to say something else, but Nannon has pulled the throttle out and turned up Water Street, and the noise of the engine is louder than anything the woman might have said. As they drive up the hill Mari turns around and puts a hand over the leather seat and looks out of the back window but all she can see are the woman's ankles and shoes sticking out below a cloud of dirty smoke.

'No one makes me laugh like you do, Nannon,' Elsa says.

'She deserved it.'

Nannon waves her hand again airily, and Mari grabs onto the handle of the car door in case they run into a hedge. They pass a house below the cemetery gates with a wire cage in the front garden, like the chicken run Frank has built in the orchard for Nannon to keep hens. Mari presses her face to the glass as they pass the cottage, hoping to see the pet monkey with his sad, wrinkled face, but the run is empty.

'It's probably too cold for it to be let out today,' Elsa says, before Mari can ask, and the way she says it makes Mari think that her mother doesn't want to talk any more, so she pushes herself right back on the seat and stares out at the world from an angle, the yew hedge of the cemetery appearing and disappearing, trees and chimney pots petering out, until there is just her face reflected in the glass, moving across the sky. On the hilltop roads there are trees with bare branches, doubled-up by the wind. When the car begins to dip downwards again, the flat fields spotted with sheep between the road and the valley bed tilt back and fore, as if they are on a boat caught in an unexpected swell, pushing them up off the surface. Before long, though, the sea of green around them becomes steady, and houses start to fly by the windows, quickly at first, then slowing down until the car comes to a halt on a street with shops all along one side and a high sandstone wall and a pair of black wrought-iron gates on the other. Nannon sighs as the engine whines away to nothing, and sits back in her seat, her tweed coat sliding about on its leather surface. It makes a rude, belching noise when she shifts her weight around, but she takes no notice.

'Shall we get to Gino's before the rush?' she says to Elsa.

'Yes, let's,' says Elsa, smiling.

The café is all marble and mirrors. There is a tall man behind the counter wearing a collar and tie, and a plain white apron. He smiles broadly, as if he's been waiting for them.

'Hello, Gino,' says Nannon.

'What a wonderful surprise,' the man says in a staccato voice. 'It's been too long since we saw our friends from New Quay. Please, take a seat by the window.'

Elsa and Mari sit facing each other, and Nannon has the view of the street outside. Mari looks at Gino's bald spot moving about in the mirror, and the pictures of opera singers on the walls, their mouths wide open. Nannon sighs and spreads her arms out across the table.

'Isn't this wonderful, getting away for the day?' she says.

'Here we are,' says Gino. He puts two small, thick cups and saucers on the table, and moves the sugar pot from the centre closer to Nannon. He goes back behind the counter and brings out a dish set with cut sandwiches and a tall glass filled with something that looks like crushed ice, with blackberries sprinkled over the top.

'And for the young lady, a sorbet made with fruits of the season. Our own new recipe.'

'What do you say, Mari?' says Nannon.

'Thank you,' she says, eyeing the blackberries as they start to collapse into the melting sorbet. She takes the long spoon which came with it and starts eating straightaway. The cold tang of it hurts her mouth, but it is moist and sweet, better than chocolate.

Nannon stirs a spoonful of sugar into her coffee. Gino has gone back behind the counter and is washing cups at a sink against the wall. Elsa is staring at the grey veins of the marble table top.

'What's wrong?' Nannon says to her. 'I'm going to treat you both. I'm going to get a proper trunk for Mari, a good one for school, and you can choose whatever you like – maybe a valise? They've got lovely leather ones in that place next to the ironmonger's. Nice and light for travelling overseas.' She looks straight out of the window down the high street. 'I think I've got everything ready for Mari, at least. Maybe we could do with a few more handkerchiefs, though.'

'I can't stop it happening, though, can I?' says Elsa. 'Any of it.'

Mari pushes her spoon into the sorbet and pulls the sticky centre out. She holds it up before putting it in her mouth, examining the pellets of squashed fruit.

'Have you finished?' Nannon says to Mari. Mari hasn't, but she gets down from the table.

'I want you to go out and get some fresh air, *cariad*,' Nannon says, getting up and making sure that Mari is wrapped up warm in her new grey school coat. 'Go over to the fountain and sit on that bench there until Nannon comes to get you, there's a good girl.' And she puts a hand on either side of Mari's head, and strokes her hair, then sits back down, holding her small coffee cup with both hands, her coat still over her shoulders.

Gino is shouting orders into the kitchen.

'Lasagna… *Cawl*, please… Open sandwich with ham.'

Mari crosses the road and looks at the fountain. The dark stone makes the running water look black, but she drinks it anyway, just to see what it tastes like, cupping it in earthy handfuls and letting it dribble down the sides of her mouth. She stands back and reads the inscription, taking her time, because some of the English words are new to her: *Whosoever drinketh of this water shall thirst again but whosoever drinketh of the water that I shall give him shall never thirst.* She puts her fingers into the letters and runs them up and down, as if she's writing them out for herself. She wonders what *whosoever* is. She looks over at Gino's. Nannon has put her coffee cup back in its saucer and pushed it to one side. Mari can't see her face, because Elsa is in the way, her shoulders jerking up and down.

Mari runs over to the pavement on the other side of the road. She pushes the door of the café open.

'And I swear to God,' Elsa is saying loudly, rubbing her face with a hankie so that the make-up runs everywhere, leaving circles under her eyes the colour of blackberry pulp. 'If I could drown it like a puppy, I would.'

'There's some would kill for a baby, you know that,' Nannon says.

Gino slams the till shut behind them and Nannon looks up and sees Mari. The solemn expression on her face stays the same, but she puts an arm out, and Mari runs to her.

'Right then,' she says loudly, her arm tight around Mari's new coat. 'Time for us to let our friend Gino clear the table and get on with our shopping.'

Nannon and Elsa spend the afternoon playing with trunks and hatboxes, exclaiming over collapsible hangers and folding handles, while Mari stands in the shop window and looks across the street through the iron gates at the playing fields opposite, at the college girls chasing a ball with lacrosse sticks and shouting at each other, their bare legs red raw with cold.

By the time all the errands have been seen to, the afternoon air is thickening into mist and Nannon says they should start to make tracks for home. As they pass the playing fields, Elsa stops to watch the girls in their gymslips flitting in and out of the shadows.

'Come on,' Nannon says, taking her arm.

Mari walks behind them to the car, putting her hand into the pocket of her new coat and touching the stiff corners of the envelope inside, the one with Oscar's name on it, just to make sure it is still there, safe, ready to give to Tommy when he asks for it.

13

She is to pretend that nothing is wrong. She is to walk with Nannon and Elsa past the Memorial Hall to Towyn Chapel. When they leave her at the vestry door and walk along to the chapel, she is to wait, pretending that she is putting her handkerchief back in her pocket. Once they've disappeared through the folding doors at the top, she is to turn around and walk back down the lane to Lewis Terrace. She's to let herself into Gwelfor, because the door will be on the latch, and she's to go straight to the kitchen, where he'll be waiting for her to give him the letter. The worst that will happen is that she will get a telling-off for not going to Sunday school. And even if they do find out they won't make too much of it, because they think it's her last Sunday. They don't know yet that she's not going away. Only Tommy knows.

'Mari!' Elsa calls up the stairs. Mari lets the paper flower drop into a saucer of water and watches as the petals open one by one. She carries the saucer over to the dressing table next to the window. Even paper flowers need sunlight. That's what Lin said when she wrote back. That if Mari takes good care of them, they will last a long, long time, just like real flowers. Perhaps longer. Perhaps forever. And ever. Amen.

'Mari, *dere 'mlaen, wnei di*!' Nannon shouts. Nannon doesn't just save her English for certain people, schoolteachers, say, or tourists; she saves it for certain moods. Welsh is for the milkman, and naughty children, and late-night conversations with Elsa on the other side of the brocade wallpaper in Mari's bedroom. Welsh is for when Nannon can't wait any more: '*Dere lawr nawr, neu fe awn ni hebddot ti!*' Mari runs down the stairs. She doesn't want to be left behind.

Elsa holds her hand and walks quickly, as if she wants to get this over with. Elsa doesn't like chapel, Mari knows that, but she goes because they have to, because everyone else does. Even Frank comes to chapel now. He wears a three-piece suit with his silver watch safe in the breast pocket of his jacket, and shakes hands with the minister. Tommy comes too, although he talks to no one and says nothing, not even mouthing his way through the service, like Frank does. He's not coming today, though. When Nannon tells Mari that he's staying home because he's full of cold, Mari looks at Nannon's arched eyebrows and thinks, *I know.*

'People have started guessing,' Elsa says over her head to Nannon. 'I can't face all the polite chit-chat. Not today.'

'Well, it's difficult not to notice. I can't let that dress out any more for you.'

'I know. I just thought that when I let Oscar know…'

'Did you think he'd come and get you?'

'No, but I thought he might at least help me get rid of it.'

'You know you don't mean that, not really.'

Nannon stops and puts her hand on Elsa's stomach, spreading her fingers out, as if she's feeling for something.

'You're starting to pack in quite tidy now,' she says.

Elsa doesn't reply.

'What is it?' Nannon says, taking her hands off Elsa's swollen stomach and putting her gloves back on.

Nannon puts an arm around Elsa's back, as if she needs to be supported as she walks.

'Look,' she says to Elsa. 'If Oscar didn't even write back, what's the point in thinking about ifs and maybes?'

The envelope in Mari's pocket rustles against the lining of her coat as she struggles to keep up. They are walking quickly past the hall. A woman in a smart beige coat with a fur trim around the neck rushes over to them, as if she's been waiting for them. She is holding a handbag made of crocodile skin. Mari doesn't like its rough, leathery surface. It's hard to tell where her hand ends and the bag begins.

'Well, Elsa, good news, I hear. You must be so pleased, after everything.'

Nannon takes the woman's arm.

'And what about you Margaretta?' she says. 'I hear Alfie's coming back next week. How long's it been now?'

The woman answers eagerly and Nannon walks her into the chapel. Elsa takes hold of Mari's face in her hands and kisses her, a long kiss that lands half on her cheek and half on her lips, and tastes of perfume.

'Off you go now,' she says.

The first time Mari looks back, Elsa is standing by the chapel door, looking around her as if she's lost something, or left something at home, a glove maybe, or her prayer book, and is thinking of going back to get it. Mari waits. The next time she looks up, Elsa is gone.

Mari doesn't turn around and walk back down the lane as Tommy told her to. If she does, someone might see her and tell Elsa or Nannon. She walks round the side of the vestry into the trees behind. She ducks through a broken fence and keeps walking. She feels like the boy in the story going into the forest with his pop-gun to hunt down the wolf. When Frank reads it to her his voice drops to its lowest register like a bassoon, and she feels safe, because she knows he won't mess around, or play tricks on her, or use funny voices to try and make her laugh. He will just read the story from beginning to end, saying each word slowly and distinctly, waiting for the full meaning of the sentence to come to both of them. He will let her enjoy being lost out in the dangerous meadow, knowing that everything will end as it should. The wolf won't eat the duck, not really. And when he closes the book he always whistles her a little tune, telling her that that is the bird's way of letting her know that everyone will live happily ever after.

So as Mari raises a leg to climb over a stile, she is excited. She raises one hand above her head, cocking her thumb and finger like a rifle and shouting 'Pow! Pow!' like the boys she's seen playing on the beach, shooting and shooting, then playing dead.

She kicks her way through the oak and sycamore leaves that lie ankle-deep under the trees, slowing her down. She hears a chirruping noise in one of the trees, and wonders if it is a bird like the one in the story, but when she looks up it's gone. Through the bare branches there's a ragged piece of paper floating on the air ahead, circling above her head. A buzzard. She's seen them diving after field mice in the orchard at Gwelfor.

Although the trees are almost bare, they are so close to each other that the branches have grown into tight knots over her head in places and she can hardly see. A streak of silver fur runs across the path ahead of her. She stops again. She knows it's only a fox but it feels like bad luck. She starts to run, her heels knocking loudly on the path where the leaves have packed into a tight layer. The trees disappear and she comes out by the edge of the road leading up to the cemetery, and she runs back along the empty streets to Gwelfor.

When she lets herself in and calls 'Hello,' the door closes behind her with a bang, but no one calls back. As she passes the parlour she remembers to look round the door at the battened-down trunk and to think, *I won't need it now*. Nannon will have to unpack it, when she finds out that Mari isn't going away after all.

In the kitchen, Tommy has fallen asleep sitting at the table. She coughs.

He sits up with a start, a look of terror on his face, the turns in the wood cut into his forehead, Mari doesn't know how many years' worth of life in this house imprinted on his face, then jumps up, looks behind the door and slams it shut.

Then he gets angry. He points at the clock.

'Where the hell have you been? They'll be back any minute.'

'I got lost,' she whispers.

'Well, then. Where is it? Give it to me now.'

'What?' she says. Did the boy in the story leave his pop-gun in the meadow? She tries to remember the cartoon Frank took her to see at the Memorial Hall, his big arm around her as the boy marched his way home again. The wolf didn't eat the duck, not really.

Tommy's face is huge and red, right up against her face.

'The letter,' he says. 'I want the letter.'

And then Mari remembers. She is to give him the letter that her mother wrote to Oscar. The letter that she was told to take to the post office but didn't. She puts her hand in her pocket. When she takes her hand out again it is empty. It can't have fallen out. It can't have.

'Where – the hell – is – it?' he yells. And then he sees her eyes following a shadow over his shoulder and he turns around. Frank is looking in, frowning, as he passes the window. His mouth opens, as if he's saying 'What?' and she hears his hand on the doorknob. Everything will be all right, she thinks, because in a minute Frank will be on this side of the door.

'Everything will be all right Uncle Frank, won't it?' she shouts out.

The doorknob rattles, then it goes silent.

Tommy looks back at her. His breath smells of cheese rind.

'Uncle Frank?' she calls out again.

The doorknob doesn't move.

Tommy moves away from her and opens the back door, onto the slate yard behind the house. Frank's body has fallen to the ground like a sheet folded up on itself. His head is facing down. He says something, she doesn't know what, and then he's quiet. A blackbird sings from a tree at the top of the garden, or it could be a robin, and she can hear Elsa and Nannon walking towards the back door, talking to each other as they always do, each one picking up the end of the other's sentences, before sighing, and starting all over again, not knowing yet that Frank is dead.

14

When Mari asks why Frank died on the wrong side of the kitchen door, Elsa says it was his heart.

Nannon takes Mari with her to the post office to send a telegram to 38, Galskarth Road. Mari isn't to say a word to Tommy, Nannon says, or she'll see the back of Nannon's hand.

They are sitting at the end of the pier, Nannon, Elsa and Mari, waiting for the men to come back from the cemetery so they can have tea in the Penwig. Nannon and Elsa look like mirror images of each other, their mouths turned down, Nannon thinner than she was, and Elsa fatter. They sit facing away from the sea, towards the three terraces. There is no sun, and the houses are drained of colour. Even the stones of the quay seem black and lifeless. The sea in the bay and the buoys on its surface are grey and solid, frozen over by Nannon's still face. The wind blows their words out of their mouths and all around them, so that in the end even Nannon doesn't speak.

Mari looks along the pier to the hotel. Nannon had said that the landlady was going to turn the lights on when the men get back from the cemetery, to let Nannon know when it's time to come in for the tea.

There is something flickering on the damp surface of the stone underneath the old toll boards. Mari thinks at first it's a reflected light from the hotel, or a boy playing with a torch as the afternoon draws in early. But it keeps on flickering, moving along the quay towards them. As it moves, the air around it seems to open up. She can hear the sea again, and the gulls overhead. The flicker becomes a shape, moving towards them, growing arms and legs in a black suit, and black polished shoes and hands that wave and a head with rust-coloured hair like corrugated iron, and a freckled face and a mouth that shouts out, 'Mari, Mari'. The head and legs and waving arms make no sense to her separately, but the voice she knows inside and out. She starts running towards it. She can hear Nannon and Elsa walking quickly behind her. She hears Elsa make a sound that she knows but cannot put a name to. As she runs she feels Frank's silver watch in her coat pocket ticking out the seconds that separate her and Oscar – slowly, very slowly – counting down until there's no more time left to wait.

LONDON, 1996

Elsa is drifting in and out of sleep, plucking at the eiderdown. Houses, faces, photograph albums and dinner sets clatter by, as if they are being pushed on a tea trolley, and she is shaken along with them, before falling back into her hospital bed.

She sees Liz, sitting on her trunk at Victoria Station, crying. She touches her on the shoulder. 'Aren't you glad to be home?'

Liz looks up at her. Her face is still tanned, although it is weeks since they were shipped out of Hong Kong.

'Is this home?' she says. She gestures around her, at the man on the other side of the platform shouting *'Evening Standard'*, in a long wail, looking all around him and at no one in particular, accompanied by the thrumming beat of heels and soles pressing past him to get to the Underground. Some people thrust a coin at him as they go, and fold a paper under one arm. *'Evening Standard !'* Everything is grey: his voice, their faces, the newsprint. If she didn't have Oscar she wouldn't be here; she would have stayed in Hong Kong.

But she doesn't have Oscar, she thinks, with a start, as the grey wave of faces comes towards her and passes her by, leaving a misty smudge in their wake where Liz was sitting.

She has Tommy, and Mari, and they are going home to New Quay and Tommy is talking quickly to her as they make their way to their platform, his voice sharp. Mari follows behind, crying out, 'Wait for me! Wait for me!' anxious and fearful.

Did he think he could buy her off with a pair of suede gloves? Elsa shakes her head again as she picks at the thin hospital blanket. She sees herself getting onto a train with

Tommy and finding a place in the restaurant car, still arguing, with a small figure standing behind them, her head down, not whining any more.

'Mari,' she says.

'What about Mari?'

It is a man's voice, not Tommy's, cheerful, trying to sound cheerful. Tommy's dead. Buried with full naval pomp in Kenya, the newspapers said, survived by a second wife.

Elsa opens her eyes. The man is sitting on one of the plastic chairs. He has taken off his camel coat and folded it over the back of the chair, but he is still wearing his scarf. The blue suits his wrinkled, freckled skin and his white hair.

'She studied fashion at college, you know.' It's coming back to her now.

'Yes, Elsa dear.'

'Nannon was so proud. Said it was all her doing. She was probably right, too.'

She looks again at the man for his approval, to check she has said the right thing, and he gives it, nodding quickly, although he looks tired, rubbing his face with the palm of his hand in one downward movement. Elsa remembers the day of Mari's graduation, the buzz and light on the streets outside the gallery, the knots of people gathered around Mari's designs. She listens to them talking. 'And what are you going to do next, young lady?' someone asks Mari, who is standing with a hand on one hip, dressed in a mini-shift made of tweed with a brash, exposed zip up the back. 'I'm going to open a shop on the King's Road, of course.' Mari's voice is young, younger than Elsa remembers it.

'Where's Mari?' she says. 'I've been trying to phone her.'

The man coughs, and puts one hand on hers. His wrists and fingers are covered in sunspots, his nails clean. She likes the feel of his skin.

'She's always like this,' he says.

'Who?' says Elsa, and then she sees him, a younger man sitting the other side of the bed. And she lifts a hand instinctively, as if she has seen a ghost, or a man dressed up in a ribboned sheet for a bit of fun on New Year's Eve, a Mari Lwyd rearing out of the night into her dreams.

'Tommy?'

The man in the chair on the other side of the bed is well-built, thick-set around the eyes, with large, sensuous lips, the kind of man that women flock to. He looks well-to-do, sitting back, one leg balanced on the knee of the other leg. His eyes are large, deep blue, and his hair springs up off the top of his head. He is too big for the room. He is wearing expensive clothes, a gold watch. Rolex. Tommy always liked a Rolex.

'No, Mam,' he says impatiently.

'No, no, no,' says the older man, his grip tightening on her hand. 'She's very confused these days,' he says across the bed, and then to Elsa in a light, jokey voice that she knows isn't his, 'It's Owen. He's just got off the plane from Hong Kong.'

'Owie,' she says. Again, the word is in her mouth before her brain knows what to do with it. She turns it around in her mind, examines it for clues. It brings her a whiff of milk, dark spaces of night-time with nobody there, just her and him, with the streetlight on the corner of Galskarth Road shining through the unlined curtains, Mari and Oscar asleep in the bedroom next door; when she creeps back in she will see both their faces turned towards her. As she gets into bed she can still feel the damp patches on her nightdress where milk spurted out of her breasts when she heard Owie's cry in her sleep.

'Don't upset yourself, Mam,' the young man says. 'I've got lots of nice presents for you.'

'How's Lin?' she whispers.

But he doesn't hear her, it seems. He's started now, this nervous, good-looking man, and he carries on as if he's afraid to stop, about his new job, his office on the twenty-seventh floor in Kowloon, his Chinese wife. She remembers eating ice cream with him in the Italian café on Belmonston Road wearing her good coat, to celebrate something special. A maths exam. With fan-shaped wafers.

'Ice cream,' she says. 'Raspberry ripple.'

He looks put out. Perhaps he was expecting her to say something else.

The old man pats her hand, and the way he does it makes her afraid.

'Will you tidy up my things, please, dear?' she says. He starts to pull himself up on his stick, the bones of his knuckles straining against his thin, white skin.

'Sit down, Dad,' says the younger one. 'I'll do it.'

And he stands over Elsa, blocking out the light. He fiddles with the clasp until it snaps open, and he puts her things into it with the greatest care: the hankie, her passport, the playing cards. As he leans over Elsa she feels it again, that tugging at her insides.

'Lin always loved you two, you and Mari,' she says as he sits down.

The man with the white hair looks over the bed at Owen.

'She means Auntie May,' he says.

Lin May. Lin. 'Yes,' she says. Elsa can see the B&B overlooking Castlemartin Common, near Ealing Broadway, the curtains from Laura Ashley and the lacquered furniture in the dining room. It used to be so genteel, when Lin put down her savings on it with a bit of help from Elsa and Oscar, but now they play garage music day and night in the flats next door, and there are locks on all the windows. Lin employs visiting students from Hong Kong to help her prepare the breakfasts and change the beds. She writes out the bills for her guests at a writing desk covered with framed photographs. She likes it when her guests point at them and ask questions. In the pictures Lam is older, with short hair. She is standing outside a house in Seattle next to two little girls with plaits and gaps between their teeth. The photo of Lin herself was taken by Tommy out on the terrace in Hong Kong, holding Mari in her arms, their faces close together. If people gesture to the picture of Wei, as if they want to round things off, know the full story, Lin hesitates before saying simply, 'He taught me how to write.'

'Where's Lin?' Elsa says. 'I want to see her.'

'Hold on a minute.' The older man holds his hand out to Owie for the pack of cards. Elsa watches as he takes them out of the packet and shuffles them.

'Fancy a game?' he says to her.

'Ooh, yes.' She sits up in bed, excited, hardly feeling the pain in her back any more.

'What do you fancy?' He seems happy. She likes to see him happy.

'Whist?'

'What about bridge?' he says. She looks at the cards, the sheen of their patterned backs, as if they might tell her what to say.

'What a wonderful idea, bridge,' she says, clapping her hands. 'It'll be just like old times.'

She smoothes the hair down at the sides of her head. They both pull in closer to her, and she smiles at them.

'Now then,' she says, taking the cards and shuffling them expertly, chip-chopping them, dividing them into two piles on the duvet, flicking them into each other and shuffling them all over again.

'We need a four.'

When nobody answers she looks up impatiently. A crash from the service kitchen down the corridor makes her think of Marge. When the door opens, she says, 'Marge, it is you. I was hoping you might come and join us in a game of bridge.'

'Mammy, what nonsense are you talking now?'

'Aren't you Marge?' she asks. The woman is the right shape for Marge, well-covered, with her hair a bright colour. But the clothes are wrong. Too expensive and no green overall. And she doesn't have that piggy look that Marge carries around with her. She looks a bit like Nannon, now Elsa comes to think about it, with her grey eyes and arched eyebrows. Although the big hair is Tommy's, of course.

'Mari,' she says, and the woman comes and sits on the bed and puts her arms around her.

Not one of Nannon's letters survived, but Oscar's telegram did. He called at the post office after his shift, just to please Elsa, making sure that Nannon would get the news as soon as possible. *Mari Haf Jones, 6lb 13oz, born 12.10 pm 1 March 1941. Mother and baby perfect.* It travelled the span of three continents and fifty years, its final destination Nannon's book of household cooking in the pantry at Gwelfor. Each entry is written in her distinctive writing, with pictures and tips from papers and magazines glued to the lined pages in places, making a swollen carcass of the notebook. It is still there, somewhere in the middle, inbetween recipes for bread pudding and spam hash.

'How have they been treating you, Mammy?'

Mari's Welsh reminds Elsa of herself as a young woman, the contracted vowels and mutations, *ch dd th*, running all over the place, the same accent. Because although the shop on the King's Road did well, Mari sold up and headed for home, back to New Quay. She took over Bristol House after Nannon died, and turned it into a boutique. Half the houses are holiday homes now, and the fields below the new road are all caravans, but it seems to suit Mari. She likes doing the things that Elsa and Nannon used to do: picking sloes on damp autumn afternoons, and lighting a fire afterwards to dry off; coaxing stringy stalks of tomato plants to grow tall against the back wall of Gwelfor, until they produce heavy red fruit that smells as good as it tastes; and sewing, always at her machine, always making something new out of the old patterns and material she inherited from Nannon. She gathers them about her obsessively, as if they might take the place of Nannon's enveloping love.

It had hurt, going round Gwelfor on the day of Nannon's funeral, seeing her things set out on the walnut dressing table, her flannel in the bathroom, hung up to dry on the towel rail, and a photograph of Frank in the middle of the hat stand. Nannon left the house to Mari, of course, but she never filled it with a husband, or children. She kept everything exactly as it was in Elsa and Nannon's time, the same earthenware crock on the dresser in the kitchen, the multi-coloured glass lampshade still hanging in the hall. From Piraeus, that was, Elsa told her, brought back not by her own father, but by his father before him. It was Mammy who cleaned it, though, never complaining, fetching a wooden chair with a flat seat that would be easy to climb up on, and jabbing the feather duster back and fore across the top of the lantern's leaded frame until the dust fell out of it onto her shoulders.

'What will happen to Gwelfor, do you think?' Elsa says, letting the cards slips from her fingers into an untidy rainbow shape on the eiderdown.

The three of them gather round her and shush her and tell her not to worry, Gwelfor's fine, and she can't get a word in edgeways to tell them that what she had meant was, what will happen to it once they are all gone? Didn't another house tip over the cliffs at Traethgwyn, last winter, and aren't there at least a dozen others with cracks and gaping holes appearing in the garden walls, spreading up the lawns, and eventually to the houses themselves? Once they have all gone over the edge, the remnants of Welsh which are all that Mari and Owie have left between them will be gone too.

Oscar's delicate face looks washed out.

'What about that game of bridge?' Elsa says, gathering up the cards.

He perks up and does the dealing, and Owen sits opposite her at the end of her bed. 'Shall we bid?' he says, and something, the angle of his elbow perhaps, or the way he looks at the backs of her cards, makes her think it might be a Sunday afternoon, in the living room in 38, Galskarth Road. Owen is seven years old, with a good head for figures already. He and she always play in a pair against Mari and Oscar. That is the way it works. Two and two make four. And the noise of rainwater gushing along the gutters and through the downpipe outside the window makes perfect sense too, and the cheese scones hot from the oven, and the hiss of the gas fire.

'Oscar!' Elsa says, putting her hand over her mouth. 'Did you turn the fire off before you left?' She always worries about the gas.

He gets up painfully, hunched over his stick, and kisses her on the cheek.

'You remember,' he says in her ear.

When the door opens she knows who it will be. She prepares herself for the repeated shock of looking at people's faces and seeing five decades rush to the surface in one ferocious surge.

'Lin,' she says to the tiny, thin figure coming towards her, holding a bunch of chrysanthemums bought from the shop in the foyer downstairs, still crackling in their cellophane. At the sound of her name, Lin smiles, as if willing all that she was and is to come together and crystallise under the parasol of those three letters. She's forgotten how to mark the character in Chinese, but it is still her name, and the way Elsa throws it at her like a fisherman flinging out his fine white nets, with a blind faith beyond her pockmarked memory, reels Lin in. She laces her fingers in Elsa's.

There is a thud as something heavy hits the base of the door to the corridor, and the tea trolley arrives, just as Elsa hoped it would. They linger over their decisions, whether to have one sugar or two, or to share a packet of bourbon biscuits between them, drawing the whole thing out, and Marge lets them, all of them, even the old girl who's sitting up in bed giving out orders like she's the Queen of England, because Marge isn't in a hurry. She might as well. She's only just come on shift and there's ages to go yet before she can get off home.

Acknowledgements

I owe thanks to many individuals, most especially John Barnie, Patsy Chan, Stuart Christie, Gwen Davies, Tessa Hadley, Patrick Kavanagh, Jackie Kwan, Jem Poster, John Rhydderch, Melody Rhydderch Emmerson, Enid Stiele, Peter Wilcox-Jones, the late Trevor Wilcox-Jones, and Samantha Wynne-Rhydderch. I'd also like to thank Literature Wales for the generous bursary which enabled me to get started. Grateful thanks too must go to Seren's fiction editor, Penny Thomas. Most of all, *diolch o galon* to Damian Walford Davies, Brychan Rhydderch Davies and Cristyn Rhydderch Davies.

I consulted many sources in order to build up a picture of Hong Kong and New Quay during and immediately after the Second World War, of which the following proved invaluable:

Alan Allport, *Demobbed: Coming Home After World War Two* (Yale University Press, 2009)

Gwen Dew, *Prisoner of the Japs* (Alfred A. Knopf, 1943)

Kenneth Gaw, *Superior Servants: The Legendary Cantonese Amahs of the Far East* (Oxford University Press: 1988)

Geoffrey Charles Emerson, *Hong Kong Internment 1942-1945: Life in the Japanese Civilian Camp at Stanley* (Hong Kong University Press, 2008)

Emily Hahn, *China to Me* (Doubleday, 1944)

Susan Campell Passmore, *Farmers and Figureheads: The Port of New Quay and its Hinterland* (Carmarthen: Dyfed County Council Cultural Services Department, 1992)

Dorothy Sheridan, ed., *Wartime Women: A Mass-Observation Anthology of Women's Writings, 1937-1945* (Heinemann, 1990)

Philip Snow, *The Fall of Hong Kong: Britain, China and the Japanese Occupation* (Yale University Press, 2003)

Julie Summers: *Stranger in the House: Women's Stories of Men Returning from the Second World War* (Simon and Schuster, 2008)

The manual from which Nannon copies out a list of directions for Elsa's trousseau is Elinor Ames' *Book of Modern Etiquette* (Halcyon House, 1935).

The quotation from Kica Kolbe used as epigraph to this book is taken from Elizabeth Bakovska's essay '*Stranstvuvanje* and Provincialism' *Transcript Review* 35, and is reproduced here with kind permission.

Elsa's reflections on Wales' geographical resemblance to a pig were inspired by Menna Elfyn's poem '*Siapiau o Gymru*' ('Wales – the shapes she makes', trans. Elin ap Hywel, *Eucalyptus*, Gwasg Gomer, 1995), and Alix Nathan's short story 'Brawn' (*New Welsh Review* 81). I'm also indebted to the artist Clive Hicks-Jenkins, who is a powerful contemporary mediator of the Mari Lwyd tradition.

Finally, I would like to pay my respects to my great-aunt, Menna Wilders, née Gillies, to whom this book is dedicated. *The Rice Paper Diaries* started out as an attempt to find out more about her wartime experiences, and although the novel is a fiction and not a reconstruction – historians and those who were there will note the extent to which I have made free with historical events, physical locations and proper names – I hope it goes some way towards celebrating Menna's unquenchable spirit.

About the Author

Francesca Rhydderch has a degree in Modern Languages from Newnham College, Cambridge, and a PhD from Aberystwyth University. A former editor of *New Welsh Review*, her short stories have been published in magazines and anthologies and broadcast on Radio 4 and Radio Wales. This is her first novel.

SEREN

Well chosen words

Seren is an independent publisher with a wide-ranging list which includes poetry, fiction, biography, art, translation, criticism and history. Many of our books and authors have been on longlists and shortlists for – or won – major literary prizes, among them the Costa Award, the Man Booker, the Desmond Elliott Prize, The Writers' Guild Award, Forward Prize, and TS Eliot Prize.

At the heart of our list is a good story told well or an idea or history presented interestingly or provocatively. We're international in authorship and readership though our roots are here in Wales (Seren means Star in Welsh), where we prove that writers from a small country with an intricate culture have a worldwide relevance.

Our aim is to publish work of the highest literary and artistic merit that also succeeds commercially in a competitive, fast changing environment. You can help us achieve this goal by reading more of our books – available from all good bookshops and increasingly as e-books. You can also buy them at 20% discount from our website, and get monthly updates about forthcoming titles, readings, launches and other news about Seren and the authors we publish.

www.serenbooks.com